TIFFANY TRIUMPH

AND THE VAGABOND

BAND OF MISFITS

BY RORY LEN PUCKETT

WITH G.J. PUCKETT

ISBN: 979-8-9864209-2-9

Tiffany Triumph *and the* Vagabond Band of Misfits

DEDICATION

This book is dedicated to the great I Am

Tiffany Triumph *and the* Vagabond Band of Misfits

1 ARRIVING ON THE RAPIDS

Hi there! My name is Tiffany Triumph. I live in the small town of Dawsonville, Georgia with my parents Luke and Jane. They are very loving parents. We don't have a lot of money, but my parents provide the best life for me they are able, and I love them dearly.

Dad is a musician. Mom teaches ballet. They work a lot, but they always have time for me. We spend quality time together as a family.

I've trained as a gymnast since I was three years old. I'm not a natural by any means, but I do work hard and have been successful in tournaments. I placed third in the state finals last year and trained hard over the summer for the state championship, which I hope to win this year.

I'm not a naturally confident person. My mom encourages me when I don't think I'm capable of competing at the highest level, which is more often than I'd like to admit. And when I'm not training for the next event, or at school, you'll likely find me outdoors. I love being in nature and spending time at the river behind my house.

I also like to shoot my slingshot. Well, it's more like a catapult with a wrist band. It shoots farther than a standard slingshot. My grandfather gave it to me before he passed away a few years ago, which makes it a very special gift to me.

I have no siblings, but I do have two Japanese Bobtail cats named Ronin and Velvet who are like brother and sister to me. They're both jet black with beautiful green eyes. They don't communicate like a real brother and sister, but I can sometimes understand what they are thinking.

I adopted Ronin and Velvet from a pet store a few years ago. They are true siblings, almost feral. I worked with them for a year to get them where they weren't so scared all the time.

Ronin and Velvet are both sweet cats. They can be sneaky and are always fighting for my attention. Both are mischievous and always getting into trouble for something. They get me in trouble with Mom when they destroy things in the house.

My cats are an everyday adventure in my life. But nothing compares to the adventure we went on with the Misfits. It was early one Saturday morning when Velvet, Ronin, and I were down by the river. While I shot up some old cans with pebbles from my slingshot, Velvet and Ronin climbed trees. Then suddenly, a loud commotion interrupted our leisure. In the distance, we could see something floating toward us.

As it came closer, I could see it was a raft with several animals riding on it. The raft was held together by logs and ropes. It had a rudder on the stern for steering. A couple of bench seats made it look comfortable.

As the raft drew near, I heard someone shout, "LAND HO!" Then there was a big crash. The raft had hit the riverbank close to where Velvet, Ronin, and I were standing. Several animals went flying off the raft and landed on the ground beside us.

"Hello!" came a voice from the brush.

"Hello" I said. "Are you alright?"

"Yes, I think so." A head peeked through the brush and fell to the ground. A meerkat stood, dusted himself off, and introduced himself. "I am Captain Brosebeer Vandicott from the land of Soam. I'm in need of some help to repair my shipwrecked vessel!"

He was wearing a yellow shirt with several medals pinned to the front of it, blue pants, and a little blue and yellow hat. There was also a pouch strapped to his waist. But he had no shoes. Astonished at seeing a meerkat talk, I fought back a giggle and hoped one didn't escape. Of course, I noted how well-coordinated his attire was.

Stepping forward, I introduced myself, trying my best to sound friendly. "My name is Tiffany Triumph, at your service."

"Nice to meet you," said Vandicott.

"Are you a … *meerkat*?" Though I was somewhat confused, I tried not to sound as if I was.

"Yes, indeed, I am a meerkat. Is that a problem?"

"Well," I sniggered, scratching my head. "Meerkats don't talk." And then, as an afterthought, I added, "As a matter of fact, no animals talk."

"All animals talk where we come from," Vandicott replied with a puzzled look on his face. Then he turned and motioned toward the other creatures who had arrived with him on the raft. "This is my crew. Harlow is a Maltese and an excellent scout."

"I'm specially bred for hunting and tracking," Harlow said in a lilt so smooth it sounded like a croon. Velvet and Ronin looked at her in disbelief. They had never heard animals talk before either.

Harlow sported long white, snowy hair and seemed to be a happy dog full of canine confidence. Unlike the meerkat, she wore no clothes.

Suddenly, from out of nowhere it seemed, a locust flew over from the raft and landed on my hand. In a tiny, squeaky voice, she said, "Hi, I'm Britny."

"Hello, nice to meet you," I laughed.

Britny's introduction was about as meek and sweet as one might expect of a locust. And she had on as many clothes as Harlow. Her brown eyes were huge and adorned with long eye lashes.

Just when I thought it couldn't get any weirder, a cat jumped from atop the raft onto the beach in front of me and said in a soft, sultry voice, "I am Alanis, Queen of Eegyp."

"Queen of Egypt!" I laughed heartily. "Are you serious?" Alanis scurried back to the raft as quickly as she had come from it. I thought I must have embarrassed her. "Sorry, I didn't mean to offend you." Turning to Vandicott, I whispered, "Is she really the Queen of Egypt?"

Casually, he shuffled to my side and whispered in my ear, "Not really. She is the queen of *Eegyp*. It's a different place than Egypt." When a shocked look crossed my face, he spelled it for me. "E-E-G-Y-P," and added, "there are only twenty-two citizens in her hometown. We do not correct her because she is sensitive."

"I see that she is very sensitive," I said.

Alanis was a beautiful, long-haired, black cat. She wore no clothes, but she did wear a dazzling diamond necklace fit for a queen. And she had an air of royalty about her, except for being so sensitive. I could sense a maternal instinct in her that would become prevalent throughout our journey.

"What brings you to these parts, Vandy?" Remembering my manners, I added, "You don't mind if I call you Vandy, do you, Mr. Vandicott?"

"Not at all."

He appeared to truly not mind and was rather jovial about brushing off my forgotten manners.

"We're on a mission on the orders of King Zirdak to find protective assistance for the land of Soam. We fear the Snardlins may overrun us."

"The Snardlins?"

"The Snardlins are a ruthless society of creatures who intend to take over the world and will stop at nothing until they succeed." Vandy's tail swirled in circles as he spoke.

"They sound horrible," I said.

"An understatement! They ran us out of Nur, our homeland of many centuries, and labeled us 'Misfits'. All because no one would take us in. When we arrived in Soam, King Zirdak accepted us unconditionally. He took us under his wing."

"King Zirdak sounds like a noble leader," I said, trying to sound encouraging.

"Yes, he is," said Britny. "Not everyone likes desert locusts. We are not known for good omens, if you know what I mean." I laughed, and the vagabond band of misfits laughed along with me.

Alanis returned from the raft excitedly and exclaimed, "I think she will do, guys. I think she just might do!"

Harlow barked. "I agree."

"Let's have a vote," Britny suggested. "All in favor of Tiffany joining our coalition and helping us save Soam, say I."

In unison, all the Misfits said "I". Not a single, solitary creature disagreed.

"Wait a minute!" I objected. "I'm no liberator. I'm just a girl." Pausing, I pulled my hair into a ponytail, "My parents are expecting me home soon. Summer is near its end, and I've got to get back to school."

ROAR!

I jumped and hid behind Vandy. "What was that?"

ROAR!

"Uh oh," said Vandy, nibbling his lip.

"What do you mean by 'uh oh'?" I asked, timidly. I stepped one foot onto the raft to see if the noise was coming from the river. Velvet, Ronin, and the Misfits followed me, pushing me completely onto the raft.

"That might be the Yum Yums," Vandy said, swirling his tail again.

I grew more nervous. "Yum Yums? What are Yum Yums?"

Alanis, hiding behind me, said with a quivering voice, "They're called Yum Yums because when they get close enough to eat you, they say…"

At that moment, a creature jumped out of the river and growled, "Yum, yum!" When it leaped out of the water, it caused a huge wave. The wave crashed to the side of the raft, pushing it away from the bank and down the river. I turned to jump off the raft, but we had already been carried too far away from the bank. All the animals, including Velvet and Ronin, huddled together on the raft. None of them seemed intent on escaping.

I thought about grabbing Velvet and Ronin and jumping off the raft and into the water. But we were moving too fast. It was all I could do to hang on as the raft ripped down the river with the current.

Vandy made his way to the raft's stern and grabbed the handle that controlled the rudder.

The Yum Yums chased us down the river. Six of them. They looked like lizards with fins and tails. Their tails were as big as a whale's tail. Their skin was dark green, and they had one solid red eye that resembled a snake's eye. They must have been twenty feet long. And they moved very fast.

Thankfully, I already had my slingshot in hand. I loaded it with a pebble from my pouch, which I had strapped to my side. With one pull, I pummeled one of the Yum Yums. But that didn't deter it from chasing us down the river.

"Aim for their eye, Tiffany!" yelled Alanis.

"They're gaining on us!" shouted Harlow.

"Hold on!" screamed Vandy, jerking the rudder.

The raft then flew into the air. One of the Yum Yums had swam up under it and lifted it with a swish of its tail. The raft made a huge splash as it landed in the river. The bow went underwater for a moment and, for a few seconds, all I could see was vapor. A mist.

When the mist cleared, I caught a glimpse of a Yum Yum beside the raft about to slap it with its tail. I shot it in the eye. Blood squirted everywhere, including my face. The Yum Yum squealed and swam upstream, splashing and harrumphing like a badgered whale.

"Tiffany, there's one in front of us!" Britny screamed, from the front of the raft.

"LOOK OUT!" shouted Vandy, jerking the rudder causing the raft to barely miss the Yum Yum. I dropped my slingshot and fell off the side of the raft. When I fell, I managed to grab the side of the raft with one hand.

Holding on for dear life, I caught sight of a rock formation ahead. I tried pulling myself into the raft, but the current was too strong and pulled against me.

After a short struggle, I heaved and managed to pull one leg up on the raft. I tried to lift the rest of my body onto the raft but couldn't get beyond the force of the current tugging at me underneath the river. Suddenly, Harlow appeared at the edge of the raft with a rope in her mouth. She dropped it in front of me. I grabbed the rope and, with the Misfits tugging on the other end of it, pulled myself onto the raft as the rock formation grazed my leg.

I looked for Velvet and Ronin. They were hiding under one of the raft seats with Alanis. I felt relieved to see they hadn't fallen into the river.

"Tiffany, catch!" shouted Vandy.

He flung my slingshot toward me, and I caught it. Almost in a single motion, I took aim at one of the two Yum Yums swimming behind the raft. I let go of the sling and shot the Yum Yum in the eye. It squealed and slid headfirst into the dirt on the riverbank. Mud and rocks flew everywhere.

The other Yum Yum positioned itself beside the raft. I saw a blowhole right below its big red eye. I grabbed the raft's anchor, a big rock with a rope tied around it, and threw it into the Yum Yum's blowhole. The Yum Yum flopped violently until it sank underwater. Harlow, thinking fast, snapped the rope with her jowls and chewed it in two before the weight of the Yum Yum could pull us under with it.

Two more Yum Yums swam to the rear of the raft raised their tails as if about to slap the raft with them. Before they could get their swipe in, I loaded my slingshot and shot one of them in the eye. It fell underwater, leaving a trail of blood on the surface of the river. The other Yum Yum raised its tail and aimed for the back of the raft.

Vandy yelled. "HOLD ON!" He turned the raft in the nick of time and the Yum Yum's tail smacked the water behind us. It then swam past the raft, upstream, and turned around. It headed toward us as fast as it could swim. I jumped up on the bow of the raft and shot a pebble from my slingshot, missing the Yum Yum by a hair. I loaded another pebble and took another shot. This time, I smacked it in the center of its big red eye.

The Yum Yum swung around and whacked the raft with its tail. The force knocked me off the raft and I fell underwater. After a little effort, I made my way back to the surface, gasping for breath. Choking and spitting. Alanis jumped onto the bow of the raft and shouted, "Are you okay, Tiffany?"

"Yes," I gargled.

"Where's Britny?" asked Harlow.

"Over here," she fluttered.

Britney had landed on a river rock. Upon hearing her name, she flew back to the raft.

I tried swimming to the raft with my slingshot firmly grasped in my hand. The last Yum Yum swam under me and lifted me out of the water and into the air with its big fish snout. I landed on its back with my legs spread on either side as if riding a horse. Loading my slingshot with the biggest pebble in my pouch, I hopped up and ran across the Yum Yum's back to its head. Standing atop its massive head, I aimed for its eye. At point blank range, I blasted the pebble right into the deepest part of the Yum Yum's big red eye. Blood spattered everywhere, including all over me.

"Disgusting!" As the Yum Yum sank beneath me, I jumped off its back and into the water. The raft drifted away from me with the current. I swam to catch up with it. When I did, I climbed in, shivering and shaking all over. I'd never been through anything like that before. I plopped down on the floor of the raft, completely out of breath. My body ached all over.

"I told you she would do," said Alanis grinning.

"Good shooting!" said Harlow.

Everyone cheered, but I was shaken. The event scared me out of my wits.

"Which way do we go?" asked Britny.

"Don't go to the fork on the right," I said cautiously, still trying to catch my breath. "That's what the locals call the Devil's Elbow. Nobody ever goes that route."

Vandy pulled out a map. "We go to the right fork," he said.

"Are you crazy?" I exclaimed. "The legend of Jimbo Knoze has been talked about for years."

"What's the legend of Jimbo Knoze?" Vandy asked.

All the misfits huddled close as I told them the story of Jimbo Knoze.

"Jimbo Knoze and his family went panning for gold downstream. Some local fishermen had been fishing to the left of the fork. They saw Jimbo and his family head toward Devil's Elbow. The next thing they heard was screaming and crying. The fishermen said they heard strange growling noises coming from the river. And they swear they saw a monster through the woods. Jimbo and his family were never seen again."

"The map shows we take the right fork. We must go to the right," Vandy demanded.

He glanced at Harlow. Harlow grabbed a paddle and rowed quickly toward the right fork. Vandy grabbed the rudder and steered the raft toward Devil's Elbow. I fell over onto my back, gasping for air and wishing I was anywhere else.

2 BUTTERFLIES AND LIGHTNING BUGS

We entered Devil's Elbow with rapids crashing fast and furious against the rocks. The little raft tossed side to side. It bounced down the river like a ball in a pinball machine. Once, we spun around and floated downstream in reverse only to be turned around again. The raft's rudder was no match for the rough water. Things got downright scary.

Several times, we slammed into rocks. I'm surprised the raft didn't break. The water had total control over it. My fellow passengers and I hung on for dear life.

Finally, we came to a part of the river where the current slowed, and we moved at a snail's pace for several hundred yards. The water became stunningly clear. I could see schools of trout swimming all around.

I've been around the river all my life, but I'd never seen that section of it. Weeping willows aligned the banks of the river on both sides. They basked in the perfect mix of sunlight and partial shade the river offered. The undersides of the tree leaves flashed a brilliant shade of silver.

The fields beyond the willows were lush and green, reminding me of a trip my family took to Scotland to see my cousins when I was a little girl. The aroma of honeysuckles mixed with lavender filled the air. The scent of apples was also hard to escape. There were so many apple trees I couldn't count them. Wild horses drank at the water's edge. Sand bars flayed out from the banks of the river like crescents pointing downstream toward some unknown destination. A lake connected to the river on the opposite side of the fork we were navigating, playing host to hundreds of swans. It didn't seem like the evil place local folklore had rumored it to be.

Mesmerized by what I saw, I didn't notice the tunnel ahead until I came to my senses.

"Heads up!" I shouted.

"I knew it," said Vandy. "Listen here! We are approaching the Jasper Tunnel." He reached into his pouch, pulled out twelve precious stones, and gave six of them to me. The six he gave to me were a ruby, an emerald, a sapphire, a pearl, an onyx, and a jasper stone. Vandy then instructed me on what to do with the stones. "When we get halfway through the tunnel, we will be able to see the sky through a hole in the roof. At that point, drop the stones off the back of the raft and into the water."

Just as he had predicted, we reached the center of the tunnel, and I could see light entering a hole at the top. I dropped my stones in the water behind the raft. Vandy dropped the six stones he held in his hand into the river next to mine. The raft stopped moving.

"Why did we stop?" I asked.

Vandy took on a look of seriousness I hadn't seen before. "These stones have a power that few have ever seen. They are our guides. They will help us get to a window of time and return home again."

"Window of time? Home?"

"Yes, Soam."

"SOAM! I can't leave my home, my family!" I shouted.

Suddenly, the walls of the tunnel lit up and the river turned neon purple. The raft spun in circles as a waterspout opened and swallowed us, raft and all.

We spun so fast I grew dizzy and blacked out. When I awoke, I found myself on a sandy beach beneath a waterfall. The band of misfits, Velvet, and Ronin were there too. All around us, I could hear birds singing, each caroling a different song as the waterfall changed colors.

I didn't think it was possible, but it was more beautiful than anything I'd ever seen. The sky was so blue it didn't look real. A huge lake sparkled from beams of sun rays. The flowers dazzled my eyes with intense color. Oak trees stood tall as skyscrapers. Green grass covered the surface like a blanket.

There was an aroma of many different fruit trees. I saw an apple tree with the biggest red apples I had ever seen. There were orange trees, lemon trees, and grapefruit trees everywhere. The scent of citrus was amazing.

Everything about the place was peaceful. Down by the stream, a lion played with a lamb. A wolf slept harmoniously beside a fawn. A rabbit played with a coyote.

While all of that was incredible, the most striking thing of all was how lit up the sky was without a sun. The place was filled with a different kind of light. A warm light, a peaceful presence that emanated tranquility in every direction across the full blanket of sky above.

There was also a building in the sky. It was illuminated and looked as if made of precious jewels. Huge gates on the building made of solid pearl made it look like a royal palace.

"Hold it. I don't understand. What happened?" Vandy pulled his instructions from his pouch.

"Something wrong?" I asked.

Vandy fumbled through the pages of his booklet, stopping midway through to read aloud. "Twelve stones… opening of tunnel… drop the stones in the water… oh no!" A sudden look of despair formed on his face. "How could I have made such a mistake?" He shouted as his tail twirled. "We were supposed to drop the stones off the front of the raft, not the back of it," he said as he fell to his knees. With sadness written all over his face.

"Where are we?" Ronin asked.

"Yeah," I followed. "Where are we?" Startled, I turned and looked at Ronin. "Wait a minute. Did you just *speak?*"

"Yes."

"But you don't talk!"

"I do now."

"Me too," said Velvet cheerily.

"They talk like us now," said Harlow.

Britny flew over and flapped her little wings in front of my face excitedly. "Yes, we just went through a window of time. Velvet and Ronin can talk like us now."

"Woah! This is way too much," I shouted.

"Oh dear. We are not in Soam," Vandy moaned. "And I'm not sure where we are!" After a pause, he added, "I must find my compass." He walked about as if searching for something, rummaging through his belongings in search of his compass. As he did, the misfits explored their surroundings while I continued to freak out that my cats could talk.

After pulling myself together, I strolled to the nearby brook and looked at my reflection in the water. A butterfly landed on my arm. "Hello, Tiffany," it said. "How are you?"

While amazed by the beautiful creature, her knowing my name puzzled me. "How do you know my name?" I asked.

"We know everyone's name here," she said.

"Well, shouldn't I know your name?"

"I'm Gem."

"That's a pretty name." I chuckled.

A swarm of butterflies joined us and greeted me, humming the prettiest tune I'd ever heard. Several of them braided my hair. Others took off my shoes and washed my feet in the brook.

"Here it is!" Vandy's face beamed with excitement as he held his compass into the air in celebration of having found it. "Let's see which direction we should go."

"I must go now," I said, putting my shoes on. I waved good-bye to the butterflies and ran to Vandy, anxious to see what direction his compass would point us to.

"If you ever find yourself in trouble," Gem said in a syrupy voice, "The Counselor will be there for you."

The Counselor? What did she mean by that, I wandered as I skipped over to Vandy and his compass.

Vandy banged the compass on a tree, then he shook it until it started working again.

I called everyone together but couldn't see Ronin or Velvet. After a moment of delirium, I caught sight of them playing with a bear and almost panicked until I realized this place was very different than home. The bear was friendlier than the bears we have back there. But I couldn't help but be worried, a little.

"All right crew, gather around and listen." Vandy focused his eyes on a pad and paper he held in his hands. As he spoke, he made some notes. "If my calculations are correct, we should go east."

"We know about *your* calculations," said Alanis with some sarcasm.

"Yeah, your calculations got us lost," added Velvet.

"I liked it better when you didn't talk, Velvet," Vandy quipped snidely.

"No one here is lost," I interjected. "Everyone here is right where they should be. Wherever we are might not be our permanent home, but we are here for a reason." I paused. Then, trying to sound confident, I added, "I don't know the reason, but I figure we will understand later."

In agreement, Vandy nodded. Then he gathered food and supplies from the raft. A road heading east led away from the nearby brook, and we decided to follow it. As we walked, we kept our eyes peeled for the land of Soam.

After departing from the beautiful location of the butterflies, I began to worry. The comfort and peace I felt there was gone. Anxiety set in. I mentioned to Vandy that I wanted to go home, but he didn't know where we were much less how to get home from there. We walked for days, and it seemed to me that we were indeed lost.

Finally, we came to a fork in the road. A sign beside the road read:

Emerald Mountain east
Trigger Canyon west

"We shall continue east," Vandy commanded.

So, toward Emerald Mountain it was.

We walked for another hour before Britny flew ahead of the us to scout things out. She reported back that she had found a cave about a mile up the road. We continued our journey until we arrived at the cave. About that time, nightfall closed in. We decided to settle into the cave for the night.

My feet ached from all the walking, and the temperature was dropping. Harlow gathered wood for a fire, carrying it in her mouth, while the rest of the animals gathered moss for pillows and bedding. Britny flew around looking for twigs to use as kindling for a fire.

Vandy started the fire with a flint rock and another stone. He struck the two stones together repeatedly until a spark ignited the dry twigs.

After warming the cave with the fire, we all went to sleep. All except for Alanis, who stayed awake to keep watch. I dreamed of my family and the beautiful place where the butterflies were earlier in the day.

A few hours passed before we were all awakened by a shout.

"WAKE UP! WE'RE BEING ATTACKED!"

Even half asleep, I recognized it as the voice of Alanis.

The fire had died to a smolder and the cave was pitch black. Everyone awoke from their slumber. I rose but couldn't see anything. Fumbling around in the dark for my slingshot, I felt it beside my bedding. Then I heard giggling.

"Who's there?" I squinted to peer through the darkness in hopes of seeing a hint of who might be lurking there. Tiny lights flickered throughout the cave. They became brighter and the snickering grew louder. "Are you lost?" I asked.

A voice in the dark replied. "No, we are not lost. This is our home."

"I'm sorry. We did not mean to intrude," said Britny.

The cave grew brighter with the flickering lights.

"What are your names?" I asked.

All at once the cave lit up with bright lights. Three lightning bugs flew around the cave, ducking and diving at the Misfits and me. Velvet and Ronin swatted at them, but the lightning bugs were too fast for their little cat paws.

"We know your names," one of the lightning bugs said.

"You do? And how's that?" I asked.

"We heard you talking earlier, Tiffany," one of the other lightning bugs informed me.

"It's only fair that we should know your names then," I replied, sarcastically.

A lightning bug buzzed toward me, hovering near my nose. "I'm Faith," she said. Pointing to a couple of other lightning bugs nearby, she added, "He is Hope, and she is Love."

"Those are interesting names for lightning bugs," said Alanis.

"Yes, they are interesting," said Velvet slyly.

"Behave yourself, Velvet. These are our friends," I said sternly.

"We must be on our way," said Vandy.

"Where are you going?" Faith asked.

"We are off to Emerald Mountain," said Harlow.

"Did that dog just speak?" asked Hope.

"I think it did!" said Love.

Now, of course, what went through my mind was that talking lightning bugs appeared shocked that a dog could talk. I humored myself by asking, "Do you not think it is odd that speaking lightning bugs are surprised to find a talking dog?"

"No," replied Faith. "Look outside and what do you see?"

I walked to the opening of the cave and was astonished to see millions of lightning bugs flitting around the mouth of the cave. The night sky was lit up as if the sun had woken. Insects on the ground worked hard at building homes and storing food in their shelters. Some of the insects provided food for the lightning bugs while others gave them supplies for keeping the sky lit up for them.

The insects communicated amazingly well with each other, but some spoke different languages.

"See, talking insects are normal in our land just as your kind speak to each other in your land," Faith said. "Have you considered that insects in your land may speak to each other, but with voices too small for you to hear?"

I had never thought about that, but it made sense.

"We are all here for a reason. Every effect has a cause, and every cause has an effect. There is no chance, just as you are not in your world by chance. It is all part of a masterful plan," said Faith.

"We know a shortcut to Emerald Mountain if you would like us to show you," Hope said.

"Of course," said Vandy.

"Follow us then," said Faith, Hope, and Love in unison.

On that, they flew out of the back of the cave into the distance. The rest of us hurried to catch up with them. We ran about a hundred yards and watched them fly into a tunnel. We entered the tunnel behind them and were on our way. The lightning bugs lit up the tunnel, making it easy for our vagabond band of misfits to follow their path as far as they would take us.

After a little while of walking, I noticed a familiar smell. "Is that chocolate?"

"Yes, it is," said Love. "We are entering Cocoa Canyon. The canyon walls are lined with chocolate. Go ahead and taste it."

I flaked a piece off the wall of the cave with a finger. It was the most delicious piece of chocolate I'd ever tasted. The moment it hit my tongue, something strange happened. I caught a glimpse of a future event that included me. I was standing against a mighty army and the Misfits were preparing for battle. A woman dressed in black chased me while a great city fell under siege to an army of thousands. I also saw myself grab my leg in pain.

When the vision ended, a bright light beamed into the mouth of the tunnel. Emerald Mountain, in the distance, shined like a diamond.

3 ENGLOW'S DIRECTIVE

"STOP RIGHT THERE!"

The voice came from the end of the tunnel.

Faith, Hope, and Love seized the opportunity to bid their farewells and head back to the cave. After all, they said, their movements most often take place at night.

The Misfits and I said our goodbyes and thanked the lightning bugs for leading us to Emerald Mountain. Once that was done, I turned and saw Vandy arguing with a strange-looking creature outside of the tunnel entrance.

"It will be fifty shiflets to enter Emerald Mountain!" said the creature.

Velvet and Ronin trailed behind me as I walked out of the mouth of the tunnel. The Misfits created a ruckus of their own fighting over what direction we would go next. As I exited the tunnel, I caught a glimpse of the majestic Emerald Mountain playing backdrop to the bickering Misfits, Vandy, and the creature I had never seen before.

The mountain was breathtaking. Made of solid emerald, its surface was the most beautiful translucent green I had ever seen. The peak rose into the clouds like a dolphin leaping out of an ocean. Waterfalls cascaded off the top of the mountain as if dancing to music. The lake at the bottom of the mountain lay like a turquoise blanket. When I reached the water bank, I saw many types of living creatures swimming at the bottom of the lake. So deep, so clear, and so clean it was.

The sounds and smells were as mighty as the visuals. The waterfalls echoed like rolling thunder. The mighty birds of the air cawed with authority. The fragrant air was as aromatic as a million roses. All my senses magnified beyond their natural abilities.

After taking it all in, I turned back toward the confrontation taking place at the mouth of the tunnel. Vandy pointed his finger at the face of the strange creature, his tail swirling like a pinwheel. The creature, with its big belly, short legs, and long neck, responded by pointing his finger at the tip of Vandy's nose. His eyes were huge and looked funny above his tiny mouth, but he spoke very loudly. He wore black shorts, a red shirt, and sandals made of leather. The Misfits were all in an uproar, and I was starting to get a headache from all the yelling.

"STOP IT, NOW! STOP IT AT ONCE!" I yelled. Everyone went silent. "What seems to be the problem?"

"He's trying to make us pay to enter Emerald Mountain," said Alanis.

"He has no authority to charge us fifty shiflets to enter the mountain," Vandy added.

"What is a shiflet?" I asked, out of curiosity. But I also hoped my question might calm things down and bring some civility to the ruckus.

"Some form of currency," said Harlow.

"What's your name?" I asked, turning to the creature.

Blushingly, he mumbled, "Englow."

After I introduced myself, Velvet, Ronin, and the rest of our party, the creature pulled an eyepiece out of his shirt pocket and placed it in front of his left eye. He looked us over and held out his hand with the palm facing upward. "That will be fifty shiflets, please."

I bit my lip and tried to think of the best way to say that we didn't have the currency he sought. After a moment, I just spit it out. "Sorry, but we don't have any shiflets."

"You cannot cross over the mountain without paying."

"All we have are a few supplies," Britny said in her little voice. "Some bread, some jerky, and some fruit."

Englow's face lit up. In a big gruff voice he said, "Fruit! Why didn't you say so? I love fruit. Come on in!"

Harlow retrieved some fruit from the supplies she was carrying and gave it to Englow. He immediately released the gate to let us in.

"I wouldn't have given him anything," mumbled Vandy, walking through the gate toward the mountain.

"Oh, Vandy, we are guests," I said, trying not to be too harsh. "We must obey the rules of the land." Reluctantly, he understood and acknowledged that I was correct.

Englow asked, "What brings you to Emerald Mountain?"

"We are lost and trying to get back home," I said.

"Where is home?"

"Our home is in Soam," said Vandy.

"Ronin, Velvet, and I live in Georgia," I said.

Englow looked puzzled. "Soam? Georgia? I've never heard of such places."

I explained the mistake Vandy had made at the river with the stones. As I did, Englow's eyes opened wide with surprise. Or wonder. I couldn't tell which.

"Now I see. Yes, now I see." After a brief pause, he added. "I know why I've never heard of these strange lands. They don't exist yet."

"What?!" shouted Velvet.

The palms of my hands grew misty from the nervous tension. "What do you mean, Englow? How could our lands not exist? We are here, aren't we?"

Englow pulled up his eyepiece again and sized me up, in earnest.

"Yes, you are here, but you have traveled through the wrong window of time. You moved through time at the speed of light. Everyone ages more slowly when moving at lightspeed.

"In that case, you are aging more slowly than if you were back in your own world. Time itself is different here than in your world. You have gone back in time. If you go back through the same window of time, there's a possibility everyone in your world could have aged forty or fifty years. Maybe more."

"But I'm just twelve years old."

Englow said, "Maybe in your world, but not in this one."

At that, an anxiousness came over me. I missed my mother and father more than ever and feared I would never see them again. I grew angry.

"You Misfits! You had to come along and destroy our lives! Ronin and Velvet and I were perfectly happy in our world, but you guys came along and ruined it!"

Britny flew off crying. I felt horrible for hurting her feelings and ran after her, but she was too fast. I spotted her at the edge of Emerald Lake, sitting on the sand beside the water. I walked around the water's edge for a little while, then bent down and stirred the water with my finger. After a moment, I built up enough courage to speak.

"Britny, I'm sorry. I shouldn't have shouted at you, but I'm scared and miss my home."

"I miss my home also, Tiffany, but I will never see home again if we do not help King Zirdak defeat the Snardlins."

"I don't know if I'll ever make it home," I said, and tears rolled down my cheeks as rapidly as the waterfalls of Emerald Mountain.

Britny flew to my shoulder, landed, and said, "Yes, Tiffany, you will get back home. Everything will return to normal, but you must complete what the Counselor has called you to do."

"What do you mean? Who's the Counselor? And what has he called me to do?"

Britny invited me to take a seat. She then explained who the Counselor is and the special mission he chose for me.

"We Misfits were sent to find you and bring you back to Soam to help us fight and save the kingdom," she said. "The Counselor picked you to complete the task. He created the universe. And he has given you the gift of a warrior. The Counselor has given you many special gifts. You will discover what those special gifts are in due time."

"What do you mean? Ronin, Velvet, and I just happened to be at the river when you Misfits showed up."

"We knew you would be there at the river at that time. The Counselor directed us and told us how to find you. Everything happens for a reason, Tiffany, and you are a part of something bigger than you could ever imagine."

"So…. you were not shipwrecked, after all." I contemplated the meaning of what Britny had just said to me. "Why me? I'm not a mighty warrior or a fearless liberator. I'm just a twelve-year-old girl who likes twelve-year-old girl things."

"There is something special about you, Tiffany." Britny was doing her best to encourage me. "In time, you will find it in yourself. For now, please help us. You are our only hope."

"I will help you," I said, rising to my feet. "But I'm not sure how much help I'll be."

We left the lake and made our way back to the others. Englow explained to us what kind of danger we might be headed into. He told us that someone would have to be an exceptional fighter. He looked at me through his eyepiece again and said, "That someone is you, Tiffany. We start training at sunrise."

"We? You mean *me?*" I almost choked on my words.

"Yes, you."

"That will be interesting."

"You have no idea," Englow said with a cloaked grin.

Without giving me time to reply, Englow stretched his legs, hiked quickly along a rocky path up Emerald Mountain and toward his home. The Misfits and I followed, with Velvet and Ronin right behind. After a several minute trek, we came to a lair perched on the side of the cliff. It was a cave with a huge door on the front, and the door had a combination lock on its latch. Englow twisted the dials. After several clicks, I heard pulleys and levers jostling about inside the lock. A few seconds later, the door rolled up like a garage door.

Two dogs waited inside the doorway. They looked like hyenas, but their fur was solid white with black spots peppered all over them. The dogs looked menacing, with drool spilling out of their mouths. And they were growling.

"Stop it now!" Englow ordered.

"Yeah, stop it now!" snarked Ronin.

I shot a laser-like glance at Ronin and said, "Quit being rude. This is not our home."

"Yeah, Ronin, quit being rude," chided Velvet.

"Shut up, Velvet. I didn't ask your opinion," Ronin snapped back.

"Both of you guys be quiet! You are embarrassing me in front of our new friends," I said, trying to be gentle.

"How do you do? My name is Tasah," one of the hyenas said in a husky voice.

The other hyena, in an equally husky voice, said, "I'm Sasah."

"Nice to meet you," I said cheerfully. Then I introduced Velvet, Ronin, and the Misfits, and we entered Englow's lair.

As we entered the lair, something strange caught my eye. The walls were emerald-colored, just like Emerald Mountain. But when I looked at them, I could see them moving. Appearing right before my eyes were movie-like scenes moving from left to right, and right to left. There were happy scenes of creatures having fun together, and there were some ominous scenes of war and famine. First, they moved one way then changed directions and moved the other.

I saw a great battle unlike anything I had ever seen or heard. And I saw a city that looked like it was made of gold, which fascinated me.

When I asked why the walls were showing me these scenes, Englow told me I was "watching the past, present, and future." He said it could be the "fourth, or possibly fifth, dimension." When I pressed him on more details, he abruptly changed the subject.

Englow's lair was very nice. It smelled like apricots. The furniture, made of tree roots and wood, played home to the softest cushions. The floors of the cave glowed with solid emerald. There were many lit candles filling the room with light. A huge fireplace carved from emerald stood nonchalantly in the back corner. Several different spicy aromas emanated from cooking kettles hung over emerald rods inside the fireplace.

Englow went to work preparing a feast. And it smelled delicious. I wasn't sure what I was eating, but I was hungry and did not ask questions. After the meal, we sat on Englow's furniture, but I made Ronin and Velvet lie on the floor, and we got to know each other better.

As evening drew nearer, we grew tired and decided to turn in for the night. Englow directed everyone to their rooms for sleeping. He put Velvet, Ronin, and me in the last bedroom down the hall. A sink in the bedroom featured continuously running water. Towels and soaps sat beside a tub, which contained warm bubbling water. Everything was prepared for us, as if Englow knew we were coming.

After taking a bath, I dried my hair with one of Englow's towels. Velvet and Ronin had already fallen asleep on the bed. I lay down beside them and quickly fell asleep myself. When a loud bang interrupted my deep sleep, I jumped out of bed while Velvet and Ronin hid under a chair.

"Get up, Tiffany! We must train now!" Englow's voice rang inside the lair. I had no idea what time it was and was still very sleepy, but I did not dare argue the matter.

Slowly, I put on my shoes and grabbed by slingshot. I followed Englow out of the room and down the hall as Velvet and Ronin climbed back into bed. All the Misfits were still sleeping in their bedrooms, separate from Vandy's. As I walked past Vandy's bedroom, I could see him sitting on his bed reading through his handbook. On the outside, he looked tough, but I sensed a sadness about him.

"Good morning, Vandy," I said.

"Good morning and good luck," he whispered.

Englow and I walked to the front door. After Englow unlocked it, the door flew open. It was still dark outside, but I could see daybreak coming soon.

"Follow me."

I followed Englow down the trail until we came to a bog. It smelled like one would expect a bog to smell, musty with the stench of stagnant water.

That didn't look like much of a training ground. Reluctantly, I walked deeper into the forest. Englow stopped and looked around. Then he walked to a moss-covered rock and pushed the moss onto the ground. Beneath me, the ground shifted, and I fell through, landing on a huge bed of peat moss and bouncing. I hit the ground with a thud, landing on a giant tree root growing inside the pit.

From above, Englow yelled, "Tiffany, are you alright? "

Startled, I replied, "Yeah, I think so."

"Do you have your weapon?"

"You mean my slingshot?"

"Yes, your slingshot."

"I have it."

Englow then explained. "Tiffany, look out for the gumdrops, and keep your slingshot loaded. The gumdrops will come from every direction. Shoot the gumdrops in the order in which they light up."

"Gumdrops?" Something popped me in the back of the head. "Ouch!" I rubbed the spot where that something hit. "That did not feel like a gumdrop to me."

"Oh, those are not real gumdrops. No one knows what they really are. They have always been called gumdrops because of their color and shape."

"Good grief," I exclaimed, feeling exhausted already.

I didn't see any more gumdrops for a while. It was totally dark in that pit. My surroundings were damp, inky-dark, and smelly. I could hear the steady drip of water. The ground was very soft. I stepped into a crevasse that ran the length of the pit. Suddenly, a gumdrop lit up green and came toward me so fast I couldn't get my slingshot ready. It knocked me to the ground. Another lit up red and nearly beamed me like the first one had. I loaded my slingshot and shot at a green gumdrop. Then I reloaded and shot at the red one.

A blue gumdrop lit up and raced toward my feet. I backflipped. On my way to my feet, I shot the gumdrop. Then everything went dark again.

Bemused, I looked up at the opening of the pit and saw Englow sitting there.

"Why does my slingshot not affect the gumdrops?"

"Throw me your slingshot."

I threw the slingshot up to Englow. He sprinkled blue powder over it and threw it back. I could not believe my eyes. It now looked like a weapon, with a leather sling attached to my arm and a grip like something off a fighter jet.

When I pulled the sling back, the band glittered and sparkled. The harder I pulled on the sling, the brighter the entire slingshot glowed. I loaded a stone and fired my new weapon. The stone hit the wall of the cave so hard it disintegrated. My slingshot had suddenly become a weapon. I was ready for gumdrops.

4 AM I A WARRIOR?

"Tiffany, concentrate!" shouted Englow. "When the gumdrops pick up pace, slow down in your mind. Remember, you must shoot them in order of appearance based on the blinking color."

A gumdrop appeared and circled around me. It blinked blue, then gold, then silver. After that, three gumdrops lit up in front of me. Brown, purple, red. Next, three gumdrops lit up behind me. The first lit up green, the second white, and the third pink.

The one gumdrop circling around me picked up speed. It flew around me so fast, I couldn't keep up. It dizzied me to try. The silver light was the easiest to see. Gold and blue were hard to see because the gumdrop blinked so fast. Remembering my task to shoot the gumdrop when it landed on the first color, I took a deep breath and counted backwards as the colors changed.

I started counting on silver. "Three," I whispered as I loaded a pebble into my slingshot. The gumdrop changed from silver to gold. I whispered "two," pulling the sling toward my eye. The gumdrop changed colors again— to blue—and I whispered "one" as I released the sling. As the pebble and gumdrop collided, the gumdrop exploded into several blue pieces of colorful shrapnel.

"I did it!"

I was so excited I couldn't contain it.

That excitement didn't last, however. The three blinking gumdrops in front of me moved in a square pattern. Purple, red, brown. Every few seconds they would go dark momentarily and light up again. They moved so fast it was hard to keep up.

I loaded another pebble into the slingshot. One gumdrop lit up red and flew straight at me. I tried jumping over it, but it smashed into my leg. The impact knocked me over and I flipped head over heels. The slingshot flew out of my hand as I landed on my belly, banging my face into the ground. Amazingly, the ground was soft enough to absorb the blow, but I could feel the warm ooze of blood dripping from my nose.

I lifted myself off the ground. As I sought to regain composure, the red gumdrop fired toward me like a bullet. I raced to grab my slingshot from where it had fallen a few feet away. When I got close enough, I leaned forward to grab it, but was beamed in the back by the gumdrop and knocked to the ground.

That made me mad.

I rolled over to see where the gumdrop might be. At that moment, a thought entered my head. *Why not shoot the lights from here while lying on my back? I wouldn't have to worry about getting knocked down again.*

And that's what I did.

I loaded my slingshot and watched the gumdrops flying above me. They looked erratic. It confused me because the flight pattern was different. They maneuvered in front of and behind each other around the pit. It looked as if the red and purple gumdrops were hiding behind the brown one.

I watched them for a while, trying to get a feel for their positions relative to each other, then I caught a glimpse of a moth coming from the top of the pit. It flew into the cave, fluttering around, hovering high above my head. The gumdrops went after the moth. It dawned on me that the gumdrops were attracted to movement.

I pulled back gently on the slingshot and fired a pebble into the air. The red and purple gumdrops went after the pebble. The brown gumdrop continued tracking the moth. I loaded another pebble and shot the brown gumdrop, causing it to explode.

The purple and red gumdrops turned and attacked me in a frenzy. I shot at the purple one and missed. The red one dove. I rolled and it hit the ground, went dark. The purple gumdrop flew toward me furiously. I rolled to my side, loaded the slingshot, and took aim. After getting a clear eye on it, I fired at the gumdrop. It exploded into tiny fragments.

Thinking it was safe to move, I stood, walked to the other side of the pit, and waited. The red gumdrop lay motionless on the ground. Suddenly, the gumdrop lit up again, raised itself off the ground, and came straight for me.

I tried loading the slingshot but dropped the pebble. Nervously, I reached for another one. With no time to load, I dove out of the way as the gumdrop brushed passed me. I had moved out of the way in the nick of time, and it smashed into the side of the pit sinking into the pit wall.

I picked myself off the ground and reloaded taking aim for the red gumdrop. The gumdrop shimmied back and forth trying to pull itself out of the wall. It expanded, contracted, and expanded again trying to release itself as if exercising a mind of its own. I fired at it. The pebble landed dead center of the gumdrop and exploded.

The walls of the pit crumbled with the force of the explosion. It looked like a thousand bolts of lightning flashing all around me.

Out of the corner of my eye I caught a glimpse of new lights blinking. They were the gumdrops that had been behind me earlier. One was green, the second one white, and the third one a blinking hot pink. I stepped forward and turned around. The gumdrops hovered in one spot. The green one positioned itself to my left. The white one hovered in the middle, and the pink one treaded air on the right. I loaded the slingshot again.

This is too easy, I thought. Pulling the sling back and aiming at the flickering light, I kept my eyes fixed on the green gumdrop. They changed colors and reversed order. Pink levitated to the left, white stayed in the middle, and green moved right.

I hesitated. *Do I shoot the green one first or the pink one? Are they the same gumdrops or have they changed?*

The gumdrops bolted around the room, circling me. With no time to contemplate, I had to decide which one to aim for. The gumdrops spun in a tight circle. Then, one by one, they split off into different directions and changed colors again.

I heard Englow's voice in the back of my head, *Slow down in your mind.* I relaxed, took a deep breath, and focused on the gumdrops. Everything slowed to a crawl. Even my body movements. As if moving in slow motion. For a moment, I felt like I had fallen underwater, as if losing my footing in a backyard swimming pool.

The gumdrops moved even slower. Their colors flickered slowly. I focused on the gumdrops rather than the colors.

The pink one, which had been green, blinked a light green each time it changed colors. The green gumdrop, which was originally pink, blinked pink each time it changed colors. And the white gumdrop did the same, blinking white before changing colors. I watched them a few repetitions to detect their pattern. Every three blinks, in unison, they would arrive at their original colors.

Suddenly, with no warning, the gumdrops simultaneously lunged toward my head. Snapping out of my slow-motion trance, I backed up and ran away from them toward the pit wall. When I reached the wall, I ran up the tree root growing inside of it and spun around, pulled my slingshot to my eye, aimed, and shot the pink gumdrop. It exploded.

The white gumdrop collided with my hand, knocking the slingshot to the ground and into a crevasse. The green gumdrop beamed my shoulder, spinning me off the tree root. I lost my footing and fell to the ground.

Attempting to retrieve the slingshot, I crawled to the crevasse. The slingshot was stuck. The white gumdrop circled around and attacked me again.

Waiting until the gumdrop was close enough, I waved my hand over the crevasse hoping to draw the gumdrop away from me and toward the crevasse. It headed straight for my hand. Just before impact, I rolled out of the way and the gumdrop crashed into the crevasse. The slingshot flew into the air. I jumped up and caught it, loading it in a single motion.

The gumdrop bounced off the ground and shot toward me like a magnet drawn to steel. I aimed and fired a pebble. The gumdrop exploded. Just one more gumdrop to defeat.

It hovered in front of me, blinking green so fast it looked like a strobe light. Before I could slow my mind, the gumdrop charged at me. It blinked so many colors it mesmerized me. But I managed to pull my thoughts together and escape the hypnotic trance. As I did, I loaded the slingshot one more time.

The gumdrop aimed straight for my head. I pulled the sling back as far as I could, using all my strength. The slingshot began to glow like volcanic lava. I released the sling. The pebble reached the gumdrop as it flickered green. The gumdrop exploded.

Pieces flew all over the pit. The ground shook like an earthquake. The bottom of the pit lit up like a great white light, spinning in circles. The light shot from the bottom of the pit through the hole in the top. The energy from the light was so extraordinary it illuminated and heated the entire cave. It was so extraordinary it looked like a deep space supernova.

Next, something odd happened. The gumdrop pieces scattered on the floor of the cave flickered from light to dim. Thousands of little pieces blinked in sequential order. I looked at the opening in the top of the pit where Englow stood looking down at me with shock all over his face.

"Tiffany, you did it! No one has ever destroyed the gumdrops before. Some have come close, but no one has ever destroyed the gumdrops in the right order." Englow danced around joyfully. "You are a special fighter," he exclaimed. "You are a special person with a special purpose!"

I thought about what Britny had said earlier. "There is something special about you, Tiffany. In time, you will find it in yourself." *Maybe it was true*, I thought. *I do have a special purpose, but do I have the confidence to finish the task?*

Englow continued to speak, "Tiffany, pick up the little gumdrops and fill your pouch. But don't pick up more than six at a time."

I picked up a few of the gumdrops. They were warm to the touch as I dropped them in my pouch. The little pieces formed into bigger gumdrops like the ones I had shot. After landing in my pouch, they blinked for a few seconds, then went dark again.

"How do I get out of here?"

Englow lowered a vine. I climbed my way up and through the opening at the top of the pit. When I reached the top, I dusted myself off.

"Wasn't there any magic you could use to get me out of the tunnel?"

"No, no magic here," he said.

"Why shouldn't I pick up more than six gumdrops at a time?"

"Because they will explode."

"Oh." I thought, *I hope I never forget to not pick up more than six at a time.*

"Why did the slingshot glitter, sparkle, and glow like a volcano?"

"It does that when it senses confidence."

"It can connect with my feelings?"

"Exactly."

"Now that we are done with the training. I'm ready for breakfast!" I said cheerfully.

"Your training is not over, Tiffany. We have just begun. Follow me."

5 THE BLACK MOUNTAIN QUEEN

I followed Englow for what seemed like hours. We walked through some brush and reached the opening at the edge of a cliff on Emerald Mountain. On the other side of the cliff, I could see another mountain range. Englow informed me that mountain was called Black Mountain.

It was the antithesis of Emerald Mountain. The surface looked like black diamonds. It was dark and creepy, and there was something sinister about it. It looked cold and depressing. Ominous, dark clouds surrounded the mountain. And black slime dripped off its peaks.

Strange noises emanated from the mountain. I could hear the wails of creatures I could not identify. Some keened from the depths of the mountain's caverns. Ravens perched all over the surface of the mountain. I found their constant caws distressing. Glowing creature eyes peered out of caves on the mountain's side.

Between the mountains lay logs wrapped in vines, suspended in midair as if they were floating. The logs spun and would often change the direction of their spin. A ten-foot gap spread between the edge of the cliff and the first log.

"Tiffany, this is the last part of your training," Englow said. "You must cross over to Black Mountain."

"What?!" I shouted. "Are you insane? I cannot cross over to Black Mountain on those logs! I could fall and be killed!"

"Tiffany, you have the gumdrops. Remember this riddle. *As bark grows on a tree, wherever your mind may be, if your mind starts to stray, let the gumdrops show the way."*

The riddle made no sense to me. Still, something told me I should take Englow's advice and memorize it, so I rehearsed it several times in my mind. Then I walked to the edge of the cliff. After pausing and taking a deep breath, I tried to reach the first log, but it was too far from the cliff's edge. I knew I had to run and jump to reach it. I ran Englow's riddle through my mind. What did he mean by "let the gumdrops show the way?"

I pulled one of the gumdrops out of my pouch. It blinked fast, then went dark. I looked at the logs again and saw something strange I hadn't seen before. There were pink footprints all over them. As each log rolled, I could see the footprints spinning with the log. The footprints seemed to show where to step while crossing over to Black Mountain. I glanced at Englow. He placed his eyeglass up to his eye and winked at me. Then he nodded for me to cross the canyon between the mountains.

I closed my eyes and took a deep breath. Then I stepped back several feet, turned, and ran as fast as I could across the hard dirt surface at my feet. When I reached the edge of the cliff, I jumped and landed on the first log. As I landed, my foot slipped. I felt myself sliding. I grabbed the log and held on tight. Then I wrapped my legs around the log and clung to it as it turned.

After several spins, I pulled my knees forward and under my chest. Using the momentum of the log spinning beneath me, I sprang to my feet and tried not to lose my balance. Unfortunately, I found myself standing backwards. Turning around, I saw the footprints on the next log. I walked the full length of the log under my feet, a difficult task since it was spinning. I knew my gymnastic skills were about to be put to the test.

With perfect timing, I managed to cartwheel to the next log, landing on the footprints. That caused the log to stop spinning. *That's it*, I said to myself. *If land on the footprints, the logs will stop spinning and I'll make it across.* That gave me hope. *I've got this.*

I counted the turns on the next log's spin. The footprints appeared every four rotations. I turned around until my back faced the next log and counted "one, two, and …." On the count of three, I back flipped and landed on the footprints of the next log on the count of four. The log stopped spinning. My confidence soared.

As I readied myself to jump to the next log, something moved toward me from the direction of Black Mountain. Three creatures navigating the rocky contours of the mountain bolted in my direction. They wailed as their sanguine eyes glowed above the fangs protruding from their angry mouths. About the size of an average dog with bodies shaped like squirrels, their short front legs contrasted sharply with their long back legs, which made me think of a wallaby.

Englow yelled from the edge of Emerald Mountain, "Surtans, Tiffany! Surtans! Aim for their throats. That is the only way to stop them!"

I took a gumdrop out of my pouch and loaded it into the slingshot. I fired at the first Surtan's throat and watched it blow into several pieces. That did not deter the other two Surtans from coming after me in their fury. I tried grabbing another gumdrop and dropped my slingshot. It landed on the log beneath my feet and slid to one side of the log, nearly falling off. A small branch caught it and the slingshot hung there. I reached for the slingshot, but it was too far out of my reach. After lowering myself to my stomach, I slid to the side of the log and snagged my slingshot before it could teeter off the log.

Rising to my feet. I reloaded and fired at the second Surtan but missed. The pebble hit the end of a log instead. The log splintered into several pieces from the impact as the Surtan lunged toward me at full speed.

I aimed once again and fired as the Surtan was about to pounce on me. It blew into pieces showering its blood and guts all over me. It smelled like vomit on a school bus mixed with that green stuff they use to clean it up. It was the most awful smell ever.

The third Surtan ran toward me. I rushed forward, hoping to get to the pink footprints on the next log before the Surtan got to me. I jumped as high as I could over the Surtan and landed on the footprints. The Surtan stopped as the previous log started spinning. It struggled to keep up with the spinning log. The Surtan fell into the canyon. Its yelps echoed off the mountain walls and faded to quiet in the distance.

I found myself in a dilemma. The next log in my jump sequence had a missing end because I had accidentally blasted it to smithereens with a gumdrop. I could only see one footprint. If I performed a round off back handspring and landed with one foot, I could make the log stop spinning. But could I do it?

I took a deep breath and ran as fast as I could toward the end of the log I was standing on. When I reached the end of the log, I jumped and attempted a round off back handspring. Nailed it!

Only one more log to go.

With one foot on the log, how was I going to jump to the next one? I leaned forward and performed a handspring followed by a front flip and landed on the footprints of the next log. As I landed, I lost my balance. I began to fall and I heard Gem's voice. "We have you, Tiffany, and we will always be watching over you."

The butterflies broke my fall. I couldn't see them, but I felt their presence. Suddenly, I was standing straight as an arrow on the log. I ran, jumped, and landed on Black Mountain.

I looked around for Englow but couldn't see him. Suddenly, I was on my own with no one to depend on but myself. All alone in a different world and not knowing what to expect next, I resolved myself to press forward. But which way?

I decided to take the crooked path around Black Mountain. It was rocky, lined with pebbles, and overgrown with brush. It also looked like no one had walked it in a while. The mountain's atmosphere felt eerie. The dense fog was so thick I could touch it. I walked farther along the path. It grew darker. I felt as if someone was following me and began to worry. Before I knew it, fear crept in.

Winged snakes with glowing eyes flew from tree to tree. Crab-like creatures scurried behind rocks as if hiding. Every so often, the trees would move. They appeared to be sliding. The leaves on the trees looked dead amid the heat and humidity. All the creatures I saw stood still. Then a heavy wind blew.

"Hello. Tiffany," said a sultry voice in the woods.

"Hello," I said tentatively. "Who are you?"

A tall, beautiful woman with long dark hair and hooped earrings made of gold appeared. Sporting a slim figure, her eyes were green and eyelashes long and thick. The train of her long, black dress draped the ground and flowed behind her. A necklace hugged her neck. From its delicate chain, a pendant with a five-point star hung like a monument to itself. Snake-like bracelets made of the same gold as her earrings wrapped around her wrists.

"My name is Orianthia," she said. Her radiant smile showed off her perfectly straight and white teeth. "I'm the queen of Black Mountain, and I'm here to offer you the chance to rule your own kingdom."

"What kingdom is that?" I asked.

"Grab my hand, Tiffany; I will show you."

I took her hand. Immediately, I could see the kingdom over which I would rule. I saw myself wearing beautiful dresses and living in a beautiful palace. People bowed to me and called me "queen." I held extreme power and prestige in my kingdom.

Then I saw troubling visions of people being oppressed. I saw the Misfits being forced out of the kingdom. I had changed. The power I held in my hands affected me in a negative way.

"I can give you all of this Tiffany, if you follow me."

"I'm not following you," I said. "I don't want what you offer. I could never mistreat anyone. I could never be cruel to the Misfits. I have a purpose and a mission. What you are offering is evil."

I let go of the queen's hand and she screamed. Her body shattered like a mirror and fell to the ground. The pieces of the mirror moved around, forming into giant scorpions, surrounding me, and trapping me.

As the scorpions closed in on me, I reached for the slingshot. The scorpions stopped in front of me, bent their tails over the heads of their bodies, and pointed their huge stingers toward me. It clearly was their way of threatening me.

"Go now," came a voice from the woods. The scorpions scurried. They ran into a hole in the ground and disappeared.

"Tiffany." I heard a voice that seemed to come from nowhere. And everywhere.

"Yes, who are you?"

"I am the one who sent for you. I am the Counselor."

"Where are you? I can't see you."

"I'm everywhere."

"Why did you choose me?"

"I have a plan for you. You must trust me. Everything I have you to do has a purpose. Not just for you, but for others too."

"I will trust you, but I do not have a lot of confidence when it comes to leading people into battle. I'm just a twelve-year-old girl."

"Twelve years old is plenty old enough to change the world. Just remember, Tiffany. As you go through your journey, always take the narrow path. The narrow path will be more difficult, but it is the only way."

Everything fell quiet. A beautiful white dove flew through the woods. As it moved, the surroundings went from black to beautiful, vibrant colors. The dead leaves turned green. The ground sprouted grass and the flowers came to life. I knew then that the Counselor was with me, and I was with him.

6 HEADING EAST

I found my way back to the logs between Black Mountain and Emerald Mountain. Thankfully, they had stopped spinning. I easily walked across them to make my way to Emerald Mountain. The Misfits, greeting me with warm hugs, yelled, "Hooray! Hooray! Tiffany's back!"

After their congratulations ended, Englow grabbed my hand and said to me proudly, "You did it, kid."

"I couldn't have done it without you, Englow," I said, stifling tears of joy.

"You are humble, Tiffany. You'll need that quality to complete the Counselor's task."

"Is it humility or lack of confidence?" I asked.

"Hmmm…" Englow pulled his eyepiece out of his pocket and gave me a hard look. "I would say you have humility all the time and lack confidence some of the time." He winked and we both laughed.

Looking around, I asked for the whereabouts of Ronin and Velvet. Britny informed me they were taking a nap. Of course, ungrateful cats!

As the Misfits, Vandy, Englow, and I headed back to Englow's lair, nightfall came upon us. Once back at Englow's place, I found Ronin and Velvet sleeping on the bed. Irritated at them for being so lazy, I woke them.

"What is that smell?" asked Velvet.

"Not me," said Ronin.

"It's me, you lazy cats! While you slept all day, I was training to be a warrior, and was almost killed. The Surtans splattered me with guts and filth."

"What's a Surtan?" The cats asked in unison.

"Never mind." I cleaned myself with a hot bath then returned to the bedroom. Someone had placed an outfit on the chair beside the bed. I tried it on, and it fit perfectly. Made of suede, its color was a cool tan, which made me look ready for adventure. "Let's take a walk to Englow's living room."

Englow had prepared a celebratory feast for one of the youths in the area who completed The Trial of the Regit, a test to see if he was ready to become a Brima, which is something like a ninja.

One of the elders told me that the Regit was a huge cat-like creature that roamed the forest at the bottom of the gorge below Emerald Mountain. The one training to be a Brima would have to go through the forest and back without the Regit knowing they were there. If they failed, the Regit could make them its prey.

Many of Englow's friends showed up for the celebration. Being the same type of creature as Englow, they all had similar features. But Englow had a presence about him that stood out from his friends. He had an aura of respectability about him, as if he'd been chosen for a higher calling.

The food Englow cooked was delicious. It wasn't much different than the food back home, but it was prepared in a very different style. The large, thick potato chips Englow had cooked in a huge kettle tasted like cheesy jalapeno. They were like potato chips but bigger and thicker. We also ate fire-smoked fish, with succulent garlic and a buttery lemon taste. And Englow's fruit spread was simply amazing. My favorite of all the dishes, however, was the kiwi dipped in a strawberry-whipped topping.

After the meal, we played games and exchanged stories about our cultures. When the celebration was over, we were all ready to turn in for the night. Then something strange happened. The fire on Englow's candles jumped off the candles and darted around the room. Each of the individual flames formed together in midair to spell out L-U-N-A T-O-O-S-A.

From the surrounding darkness, a voice thundered. "So, you think you're clever Englow, training the mortal for the Counselor's cause?"

"Leave at once!" Englow shouted.

"Do you think you can stop the Luna Toosa from happening, Englow?"

"I said to leave," Englow commanded, raising his hands in the air.

I scanned the faces around the room. Everyone looked afraid. I was sure my own face reflected the fear I felt within. The flames spelling L-U-N-A T-O-O-S-A reformed into another group and spun like a pinwheel. Then the fire leapt into Englow's hands. Englow smacked his hands together and the fire shot out in different directions, re-lighting each candle one-by-one.

"I see your power has increased, Englow," the voice of the invisible spoke, followed by laughter. "But should you put the young mortal in danger? She will die. She's not strong enough to flee my temptations."

"Don't listen to him, Tiffany," said Englow.

"I will make a deal with you now, Englow. You, the mortal, and the lives of everyone on the mission will be spared if you stop now," the voice whispered.

"No deal. You know who has called on me. Why would you make such an offer? You have no power over him. You have no power over me. And you will have no power over the mortal. The Counselor is with her."

"But is she truly with the Counselor?" the voice snarked. "We will see, won't we?"

A strong wind blew through Englow's lair. Then the evil presence left. As the Misfits chatted amongst themselves about the event they had just witnessed, I pulled Englow to the side and asked, "Who was that?"

"The Morning Star," Englow said. "He is the cause of all evil."

"He said I would die," I said, looking deeply into Englow's eyes.

"He's just trying to deter you from completing your mission. The Counselor would have never called on you if he didn't think you could do it. He gives each of us gifts. Your gift is leadership. If you focus on your mission, which is to liberate Soam, you won't fail."

"What is Luna Toosa?' I asked.

"It's the power of the gumdrops. If they end up in the wrong hands, it could mean evil could rule all worlds."

"So, the gumdrops are more than just weapons."

"Yes, Tiffany, they are. And it's up to you to make sure they never get out of your sight," Englow said sternly.

"Understood," I said as I eyed the pouch concealing the gumdrops.

After the excitement died out and everyone calmed down, we decided to turn in for the night. I slept hard after a trying but uplifting day. When morning came, Vandy woke us with a startling wake up call.

"Rise and shine!"

I rose so fast I fell out of bed.

"Vandy, it is too early to be screaming at the top of your lungs!"

"We must go east and find the window of time so we can return to Soam and get you back home."

Harlow and Alanis jumped up as Britny landed on my shoulder. Of course, Velvet and Ronin were still sleeping. Harlow walked over to where they were sleeping and barked loudly. Both cats jumped up, hissed, and ran to hide behind my legs. The Misfits and I laughed at the cat's hysterics as Ronin and Velvet squinted in anger.

The Misfits said their goodbyes to Englow and gathered up their belongings. I thanked Englow with a big hug, and he promised we'd meet again.

"I'm looking forward to it. I will miss you until then," I said shakily.

Englow blushed. "I know we have only known each other a few days, Tiffany, but I have grown quite fond of you. Remember what you have learned. Do not let fear keep you from accomplishing your goal."

"Okay, troops, we're headed east," Vandy clapped his hands. "Everyone in line. Hup two three four."

And off we went.

We didn't know where we were going, but Vandy insisted that we head east, out of Emerald Mountain. I couldn't help but admire the mountain's beauty along the way.

A river flowed from the top of Emerald Mountain, zigzagging its way to the bottom. The water from the river crashed against the rocks in its path and the overspray would lightly splash on our faces as we walked. The sunlight beamed into the mountain, reflecting off its surface, and created a prism of colors from the mist.

I saw lots of animals as we journeyed out. Goats perched on the side of the mountain ate the grass that grew between the rocks. Gazelles grazed the open grasslands at the bottom of the mountain. Bearcats rested in trees. Caracals roamed the foothills.

I also smelled honeysuckles, but it was like smelling millions of them at once. The aroma of cinnamon perked my senses and reminded me of home at Christmas time when we would smell the cinnamon-dipped pinecones Mom puts out for decorations every year. Lavender scent surrounded us and grew stronger with the breeze.

We came upon a swinging bridge made of branches, roots, and vines hovering over a huge gorge. A raging river traversed underneath. On both sides of the river, the bridge was anchored by ropes tied to two poles that had been driven into the ground. We walked across the bridge about three quarters of the way before it shook. I spun around and saw a huge creature chopping the two ropes with an axe.

The creature, short and fat, resembled a giant wombat. I told Velvet, Ronin, and the Misfits to run to the opposite end of the bridge. Then I ran the other way, toward the creature.

I got halfway across the bridge and stopped, pulled a gumdrop from my pouch, and loaded it into my slingshot. The creature stood in amazement when he saw the gumdrop in my hand.

"Luna Toosa," he mumbled.

I pulled the sling back. The slingshot lit up and sparkled, just as it had during my training. When I fired, the gumdrop hit the creature and exploded, knocking the axe out of the creature's hands. The axe flew into the air and landed on one of the ropes, slicing it clean through. The bridge leaned toward the side of the cut rope and dangled, bounced, and swung side to side. I reached for the other rope and managed to grab it with one hand, holding on for dear life. A loud pop rang out as the weight of the bridge snapped the second rope. The bridge started to fall, swinging downward toward the wall of the gorge. I slid belly-side down the falling bridge and caught the last of its vines with both of my hands. Then I saw Velvet and Ronin sliding toward me, tumbling over roots and branches. Velvet crashed into me and grabbed my head while Ronin clawed into my back and managed to snag my dangling shoelace.

"Ouch, guys! I told you to go with the others."

"We could not leave without you," cried Velvet.

"That's sweet, Velvet, but now we're in a load of trouble."

The bridge swung wildly over the river. I lost my grip with one hand and knew I was about to fall. A huge tree canopy below gave me an idea. Just before the bridge slammed into the wall of the gorge, I let go of the vine in my hand.

Ronin, Velvet, and I fell for what seemed like forever and landed in the canopy. As we stopped falling, I heard branches cracking and breaking beneath us. The cats screamed. I screamed. After a moment of silence, and after catching my breath, I cleared my throat and asked, "Ronin, Velvet, are you guys all right?"

"I think so," said Velvet.

"I'm okay," said Ronin, "but I lost a lot of whiskers."

"I lost part of my scalp, and my back. I need to trim your claws, you guys."

Something cracked. That was followed by another crack, then a loud pop. The limb we had fallen onto broke. The cats and I fell and landed on the side of the gorge. Before I knew it, I was sliding on my backside down the slick and muddy gorge wall. It felt like a wild ride at a waterpark, except for the sharp rocks and roots scratching my body. We slid so fast on the slick, muddy wall that all I could see was a blur.

We picked up speed and suddenly found ourselves airborne. Total silence engulfed us for a few seconds before we found ourselves splashing into water. I sunk deep underwater and opened my eyes. It was so clear I could see the sandy bottom of the river, with fish swimming all around.

I searched for Velvet and Ronin but couldn't see them. I wasn't sure if they had let go of me when we hit the water or while freefalling between the river and the gorge, but I feared for their safety. Unable to hold my breath much longer, I propelled myself to the surface. On my way up, I thought back to when I adopted the cats. They were so cute, so small and afraid. I told them then that I would always love them and take care of them. Suddenly, I felt that I had let them down. I caught sight of a huge rock, swam to it, and climbed up on it.

"Hey, you're on top of me," said Velvet.

"Sorry," I said, almost out of breath. "I'm so glad you're okay, Velvet."

After a moment of heaving, I asked, "Where's Ronin?"

"I don't know," Velvet said, looking around.

"Ronin!" I called.

My heart sank and I started to panic. My baby Ronin was missing. I scanned the surrounding area with my eyes to search for him, but doing so made me anxious.

"Here I am!" Ronin shouted from the riverbank.

"Velvet, jump on my back and hold on. We are going to swim to Ronin." After some effort, we made it to the riverbank. I hugged both cats and kissed them all over their furry little heads, relieved they were okay.

I knew we were lost. I looked up and saw the top of the gorge. I couldn't see the Misfits or Vandy, so I yelled. "Vandy, can you hear me?"

Echoes filled the gorge, bouncing off its walls and reverberating through the canyon.

"Yes, I hear you. Are you okay?"

I couldn't tell which direction his voice had come from, but it echoed, rolling through the canyon as mine had before. "Yes," I shouted toward the top of the gorge.

"I can't see you," said Vandy.

"I can't see you either," I shouted. "We are on the riverbank!"

"I hear the river but can't see much of it."

The gorge was filled with tree canopies and plant life that made it hard to see anything. Alanis's voice erupted through. She asked, "Tiffany, can you make out where our voices are coming from?"

"No, your voices bounce around when you speak. It sounds like you are everywhere."

"How are we going to get out of here?" asked Velvet, worriedly.

"Maybe we should climb our way back up," said Ronin.

If we were going to scale that steep terrain, it would be difficult without a rope, I thought. I could see no path up that wall that provided anything we could cling to for climbing.

"Look over there, Tiffany," said Ronin, pointing down the river. The side of the gorge curved and disappeared in the distance, but I could make out the faint shape of what looked like a stairway.

"Are those steps?" I asked.

"I think they are steps," said Velvet, walking toward them. Ronin followed, and I followed him.

We walked until we came to the steps, pushing through thickets along the way. Craggy rocks lined the side of the gorge and zigzagged up its wall toward the top.

Velvet ran up the steps first, followed by Ronin. I went up but not as fast as the cats. It took some balance to navigate the steps because they were so narrow, and there were only a few rocks on the side of the gorge to grab onto. We had to be careful lest one of us misstep and fall, and it would likely be me.

Velvet and Ronin made it look easy. They arrived at the top of the gorge before I could make it halfway. I stopped to catch my breath and saw Vandy and the rest of the Misfits on top of the cliff just beyond Velvet and Ronin. They peered down at me working my way up the rocky steps. Encouraged, I picked up the pace. But I was careful not to go too fast.

I was almost to the top when I heard what sounded like a tiger roar. I looked down but didn't see anything. Then I peered into the forest about one hundred yards away, just below the top of the gorge. Two yellow eyes glowed in the dark beyond the trees.

A creature stepped out. It looked almost like a tiger, with black hair and orange stripes accented with white patches.

The Regit.

It looked at me. Holding my breath, I glared back. Then, in a flash, it ran toward me as fast as its Regit legs could carry it. I wanted to shoot it with my slingshot, but I couldn't balance myself on the steps and hold the slingshot at the same time. I needed both hands to steady myself on the narrow rock steps.

I pushed myself up the steps as fast as I could, which wasn't as fast as I'd have liked to go. The Regit made its way to the steps behind me and climbed the steps after me. As agile as any cat, it was gaining on me, and I thought I was sure to be its next meal. Then I heard the voices of Velvet and Ronin yelling for the Misfits to help.

Moving faster, I hurried up the steps as fast as I could go. My foot slipped and I found myself sliding down the side of the gorge again. I fell several feet until I caught one of the steps with my hand, cutting it on the sharp edge of a rock step. Looking down, I saw the Regit getting closer. Its eyes had grown brighter and yellower. As it ran, I could see its yellow eyes swirling around like a kaleidoscope.

I stood and began walking the steps again, faster, my bleeding hand dripping on the rocks. The Regit was so close behind I could hear its grunts. I heard a crash and looked down to see what it was. The Regit had slipped and fallen. But it quickly regained composure and started its climb again.

The steps widened and I went faster, pushing myself to reach the top of the gorge. I heard the Regit breathing below my feet, its hot breath warming them through my shoes. It swiped a claw at me and missed as I jerked my foot up to the next step. A tear fell from my eye. I felt dizzy and out of breath. Losing my balance, I started to fall.

"Grab the rope, Tiffany!"

Just when I thought I had imagined Alanis's voice, I realized it really was her voice breaking through my dizziness to my sweating ears. As I fell backwards off the side of the gorge, a rope smacked me in the face from above. I reached for it through the sweat and the mist mingling in my eyes. Through the stinging stupor of my fearful blindness, I grabbed the rope with one hand and tightened my grip. I fell for several feet before slamming onto the side of the gorge.

How I managed to maintain my grip on the rope is a mystery. The impact of banging against the gorge's rock and muddy wall knocked the wind out of me and a sharp pain sped through my leg. The sting from the cut in my hand burned against the rope as blood trickled down my arm. I looked up and saw the Regit above me, on the steps, looking confused. Then I felt myself being lifted.

"No, No!" I screamed, moving my free hand up to the bleeding one and tightening my grip with both hands. It was too late. I found myself being hoisted up the side of the gorge toward the Regit. I wanted to shoot it with my slingshot, but I needed both hands on the rope to keep from falling.

Think fast, I said to myself.

As I rose a few inches with the rope, I used my feet to push off the gorge wall so I wouldn't scrape against the rocks. That got me several feet away from the wall until I swung back toward it, and I pushed off the wall with my feet again. That put me face to face with the Regit. It snapped at me with its teeth, and I dodged.

The Misfits pulled on the rope just as I pushed off the wall again. As I swung toward the gorge wall, I flayed my legs straight out and locked my knees, spun them toward the other side of the river, and slammed my body into the Regit. My back crashed into the side of its head and knocked it against the gorge wall. The rope moved me higher as the Regit swiped its paw, barely missing me on the pass. I looked down and caught a glimpse of it losing its balance as I rose higher. The Regit screamed and fell into the river below, bouncing off the steps and tumbling head over heels all the way.

My friends pulled me and the rope to the top of the gorge. I could see the Misfits, Velvet, and Ronin holding the rope as if playing a game of tug-of-war.

"Oh, Tiffany. I was so worried about you. Are you okay?" asked Alanis.

"A little roughed up, but I'm fine."

"You gave us quite a scare, Tiffany," Vandy said, visibly shaken.

"We are glad you made it out of there," said Harlow.

Out of breath and sweating like a pig in a sauna, I sat on the top of the gorge and, holding back tears, said, "Thank all of you for saving my life."

Britny landed on my shoulder and said, "I knew you would make it back, Tiffany, but I was still afraid for you."

"I'm so glad to be back with you guys."

The Misfits and the cats hovered around me with smiles. I sat for a few minutes, resting, contemplating how near to death I had been. The Misfits gathered up their belongings and we headed east once again. For two days, we traveled before we saw a village over the horizon. A sign in the road read:

Whimsical Village
One Mile

Harlow asked, "Does the sign mean the town's name is Whimsical Village, or does it mean there is a whimsical village one mile?"

"Good question," said Alanis.

"It could be Whimsical Village, or it could be a whimsical village," laughed Vandy.

"Who cares! Let's go!" exclaimed Britny.

We followed the road to Whimsical Village. As we grew closer, we heard music coming from the village. We reached the gates of the village and saw the residents singing and dancing.

The best way to describe the villagers is to compare them to giant rodents. They were over five feet tall and had short upper legs. They stood on their hind legs and walked almost humanly. They had eyes like squirrels and beaks like eagles. They had small rodent-like teeth and the fur on their bodies changed shades as they moved. The older ones, with gray fur, did not change shades at all.

When the villagers saw Velvet, Ronin, the Misfits, and me, they stopped dancing and singing. They gazed at us quizzically, as if they had never seen other creatures before.

"Um, hello. My name is Brosebeer Vandicott, and we are the Misfits." Vandy's tail swirled as he spoke. He pointed at Ronin, Velvet, and me and added, "This is Tiffany Triumph, and that's Velvet and Ronin."

The villagers continued to stare but said nothing.

Harlow barked as the villagers grabbed their weapons. When they walked toward us, we stepped backwards, not wanting a confrontation.

"Leave them!" one of the elders said. Two of the elders brushed through the crowd.

"I'm Strider," said the first one. "I'm the leader of Whimsical Village. We do not have many visitors, so please forgive the *appearance* of hostility."

"We understand," said Britny.

The other elder said with a giant rodent-like smile, "We are the Hakkamadoos, and you are welcome to our community."

"Thank you," said Vandy.

"We don't mean to intrude," I said.

"No intrusion at all. Join us. Please," said Strider in a welcoming manner.

The music began again and the dancing and singing followed. Strider asked if we were hungry. "Yes," we all said in unison. He invited us to dinner, and we followed him to his home outside of town where his wife had cooked a feast. We ate until we couldn't eat anymore.

Afterward, Strider asked Vandy, "What brings you to our land?"

"We are lost. We were trying to get back to our homeland of Soam," Vandy explained, "but I made a mistake, and we went through the wrong window of time."

"Talking about an understatement," snarked Ronin.

"I'll say," chimed Velvet.

"Enough guys," I said while clinching my teeth together.

Strider ignored my cats and paused for a moment. Then he looked around at all of us and said, "I see. I may be able to help you get back to your land, but I will explain later. We are threatened by an evil enemy spreading vigorously across the land. They are taking territory after territory, and they destroy every community in their path."

"Sounds like the enemy we are facing in Soam," said Vandy. "They are called the Snardlins. The Snardlins destroyed our first community of Nur, and we had to flee to Soam for asylum."

"We do not know the name of our enemy," said Strider. "They are barbaric and destroy everything in their path. We have been preparing for a battle that will reach us soon. Today, we are celebrating the final training of our youth."

Nightfall set in, and Strider invited us to stay the night. We accepted his offer, and everyone turned in for the night. When morning came, we were awakened by a loud noise.

"What was that?" asked Harlow.

"I don't know," said Alanis, sounding concerned.

The noise grew louder. Vandy said, "That's a Snardlin battle horn."

"Snardlin battle horn?" asked Strider. "Those are the barbarians' battle horns. They have been blowing them for days."

"How is that possible? How are the Snardlins here in this world, but also in ours?" asked Vandy.

"They must have found a window of time," said Strider.

"Why would they travel to this world when they are trying to conquer the lands in our world?" Vandy asked.

"This is not good. It seems that the Snardlins are trying to change history," said Strider.

"If they conquer the kingdoms of the past," Britny said, "the kingdoms of the future will not exist. That will give them a clear path to rule all the worlds."

"Exactly," said Strider.

"But why are they trying to conquer lands in the present if they can destroy the lands in the past?" asked Alanis.

"Because they have not figured out what tribes to conquer that will have a definite effect on Soam," Vandy said. "It is possible that the Snardlins have not found the correct window of time."

"Could the Snardlins be going through different windows of time building a coalition to conquer all worlds and not just Soam?" I asked.

"Tiffany makes a good point," said Harlow.

"Yes, they could bring armies from all worlds to help their conquest, and they would be unstoppable," said Britny.

"You are right, Tiffany. The Snardlins are probably using multiple windows of time to gain support for their evil desires to rule over every living creature among all the worlds. What concerns me the most is if they find the Naem Teerts window," said Strider.

"What is that?" asked Ronin.

"Well, I'm not even sure it exists," Strider said with a look of gloom. "It's a legend that tells of a window of time that is so sinister and evil that no one has ever returned from it. It has been said that fallen angels rule the domain. The legend says that if anyone is evil enough to enter Naem Teerts, the angels will show allegiance to that person and dedicate themselves to his cause."

"That complicates things," said Velvet.

"Indeed. Because the Naem Teerts window has the longest duration of all windows of time, if it exists. The Snardlins could become much younger by the time they reach this domain," said Strider. "That would mean that the Snardlins wouldn't age much because they would be constantly travelling at lightspeed."

"What do you mean?" asked Vandy.

"When you travel through a window of time, you travel at lightspeed. The place you leave stays the same. The people age the same. But the person traveling ages slower. When you return to the original window you came from, the people you left behind could be much older, or possibly have passed on."

My heart sank as Strider's words sunk in. Alanis looked at me with concern. I think she read the expression on my face and saw the sadness that I couldn't hide. All I could think about was returning home only to find that my parents had died.

Strider gathered the elders. One of the chief elders told us where he thought the window of time could be.

"I've seen strange, bright-spinning lights at the mouth of Skull Cave. The lights will show up and then disappear," he said.

"Zanter, is there any special time of the day this happens?" I asked.

"No, I have seen the lights at daylight and at night."

"Let's look for the lights then," said Britny.

Strider asked us to stay one more day before heading out on our journey. We had planned to leave in the morning, but that changed quickly.

7 FROM ENMITY TO FRIENDSHIP

"Hey, let me in!" came a voice from outside the front door.

"Who goes there?" said Strider.

"I'm here to help you," the voice said.

"What is your name?" I asked.

"My name is Allasso. I'm a sergeant in the Snardlin Army."

"Grab your weapons," said Strider.

"We are being attacked," said Alanis.

"I'm not attacking you! I'm trying to help you! Let me in!"

"Prepare to fire," said Harlow.

At once the door flew off the hinges and a huge beast stuck his head inside. The beast looked like a man with hair all over his body. He towered over everyone and pierced the room with his fiery eyes. A small horn protruded from the center of his forehead. His hair, pulled back in a ponytail, covered the full length of his back. The muscles in his arms flexed on their own as if breathing when he spoke. His baritone voice carried a weight of its own even with its subtle delivery. "Now, if I were here to harm you, don't you think I'd have done that by now?"

He stood in the doorway with his chest barreled out, his arms hanging beside his mountainous body, and a smirky smile so awkward it didn't seem like a smile. He showed no signs of aggression.

"He makes a good point," said Britny.

"Yeah, he does," said Ronin.

"Very well, come in," said Strider cautiously.

He stepped inside Strider's home, lowered his head, and squatted to keep from banging the ceiling. We introduced ourselves and Allasso explained that he had deserted from the Snardlin Army, claiming to be on the run. He said he had gone from village to village to warn of the Snardlins' impending doom. He also told us he had grown disenchanted with the Snardlin cause and didn't want to be part of it anymore.

"How did you get here in this world?" I asked.

"We found a window of time by accident while searching for the Luna Toosa."

No sooner had he said "Luna Toosa" than we heard a commanding voice shout from outside.

"Allasso! Come out here, you traitor, and meet your doom!"

"They're here." Allasso stood upright, banging his head on the ceiling. He left an imprint where the back of his head contacted the ceiling of Strider's home. He rubbed the spot on his head and continued. "General Vot and the Snardlin Army are here. You will all be destroyed. There is no way you can fight the Snardlins and win."

"Come out and fight!" General Vot shouted.

"What are we to do?" asked Vandy.

"There's a trail behind the village that leads to the Valley of Dan," Strider said. "We could leave that way and not be detected."

"The trail it is," said Allasso.

Strider gathered the villagers that had snuck through an old mining tunnel running through the center of town. This allowed our gang to get past the Snardlins. Allasso gathered the weapons he had hidden just outside Strider's home as General Vot moved his Snardlin units into battle positions.

It was obvious that Allasso deserting the Snardlin Army was a serious offense for the Snardlins. As they waged their attack on the village, destroying and burning everything in their path in search of Allasso, our crew ran the trail out of the village. Allasso led the way, followed by Strider, Velvet and Ronin, the Misfits, some of the Hakkamadoos, and me. Vandy pulled up the tail end. As we bolted out of the village, running as fast as we could, we could hear the village being destroyed behind us. Many of the Hakkamadoos wept as they deserted their homes. I looked back and saw massive fires burning the town. As awful as it was, it did give us extra time to get ahead of the Snardlins.

The trail narrowed as we ran. One of the Hakkamadoos asked, "Where are we going?"

"We must go to the window of time and leave this world," Allasso responded, huffing for loss of breath.

"We can't leave our world," Strider argued. "We've been here for many generations. Our ancestors worked for hundreds of years to build our city."

"You must leave now. You can't stay and fight the Snardlins," said Alanis.

"She's right," I said. "Leaving this world right now is the only way to avoid the destruction of your citizens."

"I suppose you're right," said Strider sadly.

Vandy agreed. "If we do not do as Allasso says, we will all be destroyed, and there will be no one to help stop them once they reach Soam."

On that, we continued along the path and followed Allasso's instructions. We traveled all day without resting. The more we walked, the deeper we moved into the forest. Fog hovered over the ground where we stepped, the air became chilly, and the ground grew swampy and wet.

Near evening time, we came upon a cave shaped like a skull.

"That's it," said Zanter. "That's the cave I was telling you about."

Allasso stopped walking. "Yes, he's correct," he said. "This is the cave of the window of time."

Suddenly, lights started flashing in a circle inside the cave.

"We must enter two at a time. When you enter, move quickly. Once you come out the other side, move out of the way as fast as you can. We will all exit in the same spot," Allasso said.

Behind us, we heard the blast of a Snardlin battle horn. In the distance, we could see their army maneuvering through the foggy forest. Vandy stepped aside and pushed us toward the cave, ordering us with each shove as we passed, "Go. Go. Everyone, two-by-two."

As we were about to enter the window of time, one of the Snardlins made his way to the cave. Allasso ran to the cave opening to fight the beast. He commanded me to run into the cave. As I entered the cave, I could hear more Snardlins attacking Allasso. I ordered everyone to step into the window of time then ran back to help Allasso. Standing at the entrance of the cave, I loaded a gumdrop into my slingshot.

"Luna Toosa!" A Snardlin shouted amid the melee, pointing at the gumdrop and blinking slingshot. As the Snardlins focused on the gumdrop in my slingshot, Allasso managed to break free of the grip on his neck. I fired and smacked a Snardlin in the face. The gumdrop exploded and took out three other Snardlins, as well. Allasso and I dove through the window of time as the last Snardlin fell to the ground.

Moving through the window of time was different than the previous windows of time we had traveled through. We did not spin around. We moved in a straight line, and so fast that I could see flashes of light accompanied by waves of moving images. Past events flashed before my eyes. Ancient civilizations appeared and disappeared. We moved so fast that I felt as if I had been separated from my body. Strange images popped up in front of me and vanished before I could make out what they were, and equally strange noises blasted my ears with bombastic acoustic sounds unfamiliar to me.

Finally, we slowed, and I caught my breath. I don't remember taking a single breath while moving through the window of time. It happened so quickly it felt like riding a roller coaster and the ending felt like the sudden jerk and slow grind to a dead stop one often finds on amusement park rides. The dead stop ended with us blasting through a dark hole and spurting out the other side with a jolt ending with a thump. And we found ourselves lying on a pile of shouting animals.

"Ouch!" yelled Alanis.

"You're on top of me!" howled Harlow.

"I told you to move away from the window," Allasso countered. After we stood and dusted ourselves off, Allasso chastised, "You guys had some time to wait for Tiffany and me to arrive through the window, but you still couldn't get out of the way?"

"Oh, we forgot about that part," Harlow snorted.

"Where are we?" asked Strider.

"Is this Trav?" Vandy asked.

"Yes, we are in Trav," said Allasso. Confused, we found ourselves in a different world where nothing was familiar to us anymore. It was the first time the Hakkamadoos had traveled through a window of time, so they were really confused.

"What is Trav?" I asked.

"Trav is a territory south of Soam," Vandy responded. "As you can see, it is a desert wasteland, not the ideal path to our destination. But it is the only way."

"Let's go," said Allasso. "We only have an hour before General Vot and the Snardlins come through the window of time."

As we continued to press our way to Soam, my thoughts trailed off and I found myself wishing I were home in the comfort of my parents' arms. My feet grew tired and throbbed from the pain of so much walking. It grew warmer and I almost fainted a couple of times from the heat, but in time, I forgot about discomforts and focused my energies on the mission the Counselor had given me.

8 THE ALBATROSS

"It is so hot," Alanis groaned.

"My fur is burning," Ronin complained.

"This desert is not the place for cats," bemoaned Velvet.

The ground shook. And shook again.

"Is it me or is the ground moving?" whispered Harlow.

"The ground is moving," Vandy said. "Oh, there is one thing I forgot about in the Trav desert."

"What is that?" I asked.

"Sand livids."

I was afraid to ask but couldn't help myself. "I understand the part about the sand," I said, "but what is a livid?"

A rumble rose from underneath our feet. Suddenly, an explosion sent grains of sand flying a hundred feet into the air.

"Okay, I get the livid part now. Run!" And we ran as fast as we could.

The sand livids blasted through the ground behind us. I stopped and turned around to look. They appeared to me like giant worms with teeth. They made the most awful noises as they slithered across the desert sand on their wormy bellies. As we attempted to escape the livids, I caught a glimpse of shadows from above. They drew nearer until I found myself being lifted off the ground. Velvet and Ronin jumped on me, latching themselves to my head and back. As Ronin clawed my back, I felt the talons of a giant bird holding me by the shoulders and saw the ground below getting smaller by the second.

"Help!" yelled Harlow.

I couldn't help. A rookery of albatrosses below snatched up Vandy and the rest of the Misfits along with the Hakkamadoos while Allasso attempted to fight the livids alone.

One of the livids grabbed Allasso and pulled him under the sand. By that time, I was so high in the air the desert sand was but a blip in my eye. I considered my slingshot, but if I shot the bird while in flight, I knew I would perish. As would Velvet and Ronin.

"Do not fear," a voice from above said. "We are here to help. We are taking you to a safe place. You'll never survive here in the desert."

"But you are an albatross," I squealed. "I thought you lived by the sea."

"Look ahead."

I averted my eyes to the front and saw where the albatross was headed, toward a clear blue sea. The air cooled, and I could smell salt. As we crossed over the water, I could see creatures swimming beneath the surface of the sea. After a short time, I saw sandy beaches white as snow, and we descended. The albatrosses flew close to the ground and released their grip on us, dropping us to the ground. We landed on our feet and watched as some of the birds flew off into the distance.

The albatross that had rescued me landed on the beach and said, "My name is Abby. What is yours?"

"My name is Tiffany," I said, still not sure whether albatrosses were things to be trusted. "These are my cats, Velvet and Ronin. Over there are Strider and the Hakkamadoos from Whimsical Village. And this gang of folks," I said, pointing to the Misfits, "are the Misfits from Soam."

"Soam." The albatross repeated the name as if confirming what she had heard.

"Soam is where we are from, and I think we should head east," Vandy said, stepping forward.

"Yes, Soam is east," Abby nodded. "But the Snardlins conquered Soam nearly fifty years ago."

"Fifty years!" I found myself as surprised by the proclamation as by the possibility.

"Strider, you were right. We have aged very slowly," Vandy said with disappointment.

"Yes, I'm afraid so," Strider agreed.

"Englow said that if we go through the wrong window of time, we would lose even more time," said Velvet.

I thought about the difference between entering the first window of time and the one we had just entered. The first one we entered was fast, but we also spun around a few times. The second window was fast, but we moved in a straight line. I thought, *how much time have I lost back home? Will I ever see my family again?* The thought caused me to worry again.

"We are too late," Britny said sorrowfully.

"First, we were forced out of our native land. Now we have lost our adoptive land too," Alanis cried.

"I have let everyone down." Vandy lowered his head. "I was put in charge by King Zirdak to save Soam and I have failed."

"You did the best you could," said Harlow.

"Vandy, we do not feel you let us down," Alanis said, trying to sound encouraging. "This was a big task, and sometimes things don't work out as we plan."

"Have you thought that this might be the Counselor's plan?" asked Abby.

"What do you mean?" I interjected.

"You can still save Soam, but in a different way. You are all here for a reason. You were brought together for the same cause." As Abby spoke, her wings crossed her breasts. She folded them over each other in the same way humans often lock their fingers. "There is a king planning to overthrow the Snardlins. He's not a part of the Soamite culture, but he was called by the Counselor to help the Soamite people get their homeland back."

"Do you mean we should join forces with this king?" I asked.

"Yes, that is exactly what I think you should do."

"I don't know, Abby," I retorted. "I'm really confused about everything right now. I need some time alone."

"I understand, Tiffany. It sounds like you've been through a lot."

I walked to the seashore and contemplated everything that had happened since joining the Misfits. If I was supposed to help save Soam, why had things become so complicated? I sat on the beach and let my thoughts wander to a future I was yet to see. Was I brought here only to be defeated before Soam could be saved? Why did the Counselor call me only to watch me fail? If I make it back home, will my parents be old, or dead?

As I pondered, someone spoke, interrupting my thoughts, breaking through my feelings of inadequacy.

"Tiffany, do not despair. I am with you. Do not lose Hope. You have not failed. Things do not always go as you might think they should, but if you trust me, I will ensure things turn out for the best."

"Counselor, is that you?"

"Yes, I am here."

"Where are you? Are you in the sea? Are you a fish?"

"I am everywhere, but most importantly, I am in you."

"That's how you speak to me. From inside?"

"Affirmative." The voice changed to commanding. "Listen. The albatrosses will take you to meet Drakkar the Great. I sent him to defeat the Snardlins and bring the citizens of Soam back to their homeland. He will need your help, along with the Misfits and the Hakkamadoos. Every one of you has a purpose in liberating Soam."

"Will I ever make it home again?" I asked.

The Counselor did not reply. I waited for a response, but something inside me said that my question had been answered, though I never heard the response. I stood and made my way back to the others. Darkness was approaching and everyone seemed weary of traveling.

"We will take you to meet Drakkar the Great in the morning," Abby said. "We used most of our energy flying through the desert with no wind. We albatrosses are used to sea winds, which help us glide without the effort of our wings. For now, we will fly back to our nest on the cliffs and return at daybreak."

After telling us there were caves nearby that would provide a safe place for sleeping, informing us that the birds had provided fish and fruit for us to eat, and pointing us to where we could find wood for building a fire, Abby bowed and wished us good night. We thanked her as she flew off to join his albatross friends in their nests.

As evening grew nearer, we began to wonder what happened to Allasso. Did he make it out of the sand livid fight alive? We were grieved about him not being there with us. He had helped us, and we knew he was good. He had risked his life when he didn't have to.

After a short search, we found the cave Abby had mentioned and settled in for the night. It was very clean. A breeze blew through, keeping us cool all night long. Located on a small cliff, it proved to be a great place to hide from unwanted guests. Vandy built a fire and cooked the fish Abby had left us. We ate until we were full. As dark fell upon us, I spread a blanket on the cave floor and lay on it. Velvet, Ronin, and Alanis joined me, and we all drifted to sleep so fast I'm not sure whose eyes closed first.

"Ouch! Help! I can't get it off"!

I awoke to find Harlow running around outside the cave. I ran to see what it was that had disturbed her and found a sand crab. It had a claw clamped onto Harlow's nose. A common practice of sniffing holes in the ground finally came around to bite her. I laughed, as did the rest of the crew, and removed the crab from Harlow's nose very carefully with my hands while trying to avoid causing Harlow any more pain.

While Harlow woke us a little too early, the bright side was that daylight had broken through. We had breakfast and worked on getting organized for the day. Abby and the albatrosses flew in, landing on the cliffs where we were gathering.

Abby explained that the flight to Soam would be a long one. The albatrosses each lowered one wing to the ground and invited us to climb onto their backs. Velvet, Ronin, and I climbed aboard Abby again, and off we went. The birds soared into the sky with incredible speed.

"Woohoo!" yelled Vandy, holding on tight.

I enjoyed the flight. We flew for a long time, and I could see everything below for miles around. The birds seemed to sleep in mid-flight. They were awesome gliders, rarely flapping their wings. We were in the air all day.

It began to turn dark as we approached a mountain range. The skies were an amber-orange color as the sun set behind us. As we flew, I could feel the presence of evil. I couldn't figure out why, but something didn't seem right.

"Hold on," Abby warned. "I see a rookery of lunds over the ridge to our right."

I turned my eyes to my right and saw a silhouette of what appeared to be a raggedy bird. The bird's eyes glowed like the eyes of the winged snakes on Black Mountain. With a closer look, I saw a rider on its back. It looked like a woman wearing a black cape.

The lunds headed toward us from the opposite direction. I reached for my slingshot and loaded it as Vandy yelled, "Prepare for battle!"

The caped woman on the lead lund made a familiar sound. Then I recognized her. She was Orianthia, the queen of Black Mountain. The albatrosses turned to face the approaching lunds and picked up speed. Abby yelled over her shoulder, "Hold on tight. We are going to dive."

And what a dive! I could barely hold on because we were going so fast.

When we reached the rookery of lunds, the albatrosses were positioned above them and swiped at the lunds with their talons, swatting some of them out of the sky.

Two lunds quickly flew to the right side of us in the same direction we were traveling. I aimed and fired at one of them. It fell like a rock.

"Hold on, Tiffany!" Abby shouted.

Too late. Orianthia swooped down from the opposite side of Abby and swept me into her arms. I had no time to react. As she pulled away from Abby's left side, I yelled to Velvet and Ronin, "Jump to Abby!" They obeyed and I watched as Abby put distance between them and me. My heart sunk. Being separated from the cats made me think of how awful it would be if I never saw them again.

"Hold on, Tiffany," Vandy shouted. "We are coming to the rescue."

The lunds were too fast for the albatrosses weighed down by their extra loads. Being bigger birds, they had much more weight to carry without the added baggage we gave them. I wanted to shoot the bird carrying me, but that would be suicide. Even shooting the queen would result in an explosion so close it would take out the bird and me. A line of cliffs stretched over the sea ahead and it appeared the lund was heading straight for them. A tree limb extended outward from one of the rocks on the cliff. If I could get close enough, I could jump and grab the limb.

I envisioned how I would do it. If I could time it just right, I could grab the limb like a parallel bar and do a tap swing leading into a back flip, and dismount onto one of the albatrosses chasing the lund. I had performed that move hundreds of times in practice and competitions, but this was not a gymnastics competition.

"Follow me and I will give you everything you want," Orianthia whispered in my ear.

"I will not follow you anywhere," I whispered back.

The lund flew close enough to the cliff and the protruding tree limb. Just as it swerved to fly back out to sea, I jumped. Tempted to close my eyes, I reached for the limb with both arms outstretched. The palms of my hand landed on the tree limb, and I wrapped my fingers around it, palms sweating with nervousness. The momentum from my jump propelled me under and over the tree limb. As I stood on my hands above the tree limb, I could see the shadow of a bird on the rocks of the cliff. As I rounded the tree limb near the bottom of my swing, I dismounted and made a perfect landing on the bird in midflight. I felt so proud. Then I realized I had landed on the wrong bird as I caught a glimpse of Abby on my right side.

"Jump!" Abby screamed.

Velvet and Ronin, misunderstanding Abby's intent, jumped and landed on the lund I had mounted. One on my head and the other on my back, claws scratching my head and back as they held on for dear life.

Orianthia had turned and was headed straight for us. Another lund was in hot pursuit from behind. I caught sight of something out of the corner of my eye. Vandy.

He shouted, "Jump, Tiffany! Jump!"

With Velvet and Ronin in tow, I loosened my grip on the lund's neck and leapt toward Vandy and the albatross he was riding. We landed and slid. I couldn't hold on. A Hakkamadoo flew by on the wing of an albatross, grabbed my arm, and pulled us to safety.

"Thank you," I said.

"There she comes," said Ronin, climbing up my back to join Velvet on my head.

Orianthia headed directly for us again. I loaded my slingshot and fired a gumdrop at her. The gumdrop hit the bird and exploded. Orianthia jumped and fell until a lund snatched her from the sky. She screamed and shook her fist at me as she swore, "Tiffany, I will have you under my power one day!" And as she disappeared into the darkness she cackled and howled in mad delight.

I took a deep breath and gathered my thoughts. I was at ease that Ronin and Velvet were with me again. Being on the albatross with Vandy reminded me of how we were all in it together and how loyal everyone was to each other. At that point in the journey, our bonds seemed inseparable.

The albatrosses all fell in line behind Abby once again. We flew through the night without incident. When the sun rose, I could see land ahead in the distance.

"Is that Soam?" I asked Vandy as we drew closer.

"Yes, it is," he said. "We finally made it. We couldn't have done it without you, Tiffany. Now I know why your last name is Triumph."

"Um, Vandy."

"Yes, Tiffany?"

"My real last name isn't Triumph. It's Bumbleseed." Velvet and Ronin laughed. "I thought Triumph sounded better than Bumbleseed, so I lied."

"Be that as it may, you have definitely earned your new last name." Vandy smiled and we prepared for our landing in Soam.

9 PAROUSIA
(THE KING IS COMING)

The albatrosses descended over Soam and landed on an open field. There wasn't much vegetation, but it was very hot. Hotter even than the desert.

"It's good to be home." said Alanis, dismounting her albatross.

"So, this is your home." Strider looked impressed as he climbed off the albatross he'd been riding. "It reminds me of my homeland."

Vandy pulled out his compass and announced, "We still have a lot of traveling to get to the city. It is north of here. Therefore, we travel north." He pointed for extra effect.

Abby informed us she and the other albatrosses wouldn't be able to take us any farther because they needed rest from the desert heat. It had been a long and hot flight, after all.

I looked around. My face must have revealed my feelings because Britny landed on my shoulder and, in her soft, sultry voice, said, "Tiffany, I know you miss your home. You have come a long way to help us, and we love you for it. You are involved in something far greater than you could ever imagine."

I knew she was right. It was my calling to help the Misfits. I stuffed my feelings aside and focused on what the Counselor had asked me to do. What we had been through so far was nothing compared to what we would soon face. I didn't have much confidence in my abilities before, but I felt stronger than ever after having gone through so many tests and hoped that my lack of confidence would not come back to haunt me later.

We all checked our weapons and supplies. The Hakkamadoos had packed plenty of dried goods to eat. There were sixty of them in our unit and most of them were the villagers we had saved along with Allasso, who was no longer counted among our number. I felt good knowing Strider and most of the Hakkamadoos were well-trained fighters.

Vandy led us into the wilderness of the unbearably hot desert. We traveled for about an hour and came upon some valuables that appeared to be left behind by someone. There were piles of beautifully carved figurines, silver plates and cups, and a lot of purple linens.

"Why was all this valuable stuff left here?" Velvet asked in awe.

"I don't know," screeched Ronin.

"Why don't you know? You know everything else," Velvet snarked.

"You are getting on my nerves, Velvet!" Ronin returned sharply.

"Enough, you guys!" I scowled.

"I see movement over there," barked Harlow in her happy voice.

A flock of sheep roamed near the sea. When we approached them, they ran and hid behind their tents. Slowly, I approached the sheep and said, "Please don't run from us. We mean you no harm."

"We are following King Arista's orders," a sheep said in a whiny cant. "Please don't harm us."

"We are not here to harm you. Some of us are from this land also," Alanis said proudly. "We are here on the orders of King Zirdak to help save Soam," said Harlow.

Another voice interjected from one of the tents. "King Zirdak? What do you mean by King Zirdak? We haven't heard from him since he was taken captive nearly fifty years ago. The kingdom of Soam is over. It has been destroyed."

A small sheep came out of the tent and said, "I'm Rosa. From Soam."

Rosa was adorable. She had the sweetest face and dazzling blue eyes, with a euphonic voice. Her wool was thick and white.

We all introduced ourselves as more sheep came out of tents. I wondered whether King Zirdak was there and, if so, why was I there? The situation confused me.

"We hear of a great warrior that is coming to help us restore Soam," said one of the sheep. Suddenly, I felt proud. Was he speaking of me? Am I that well known already? "His name is Drakkar the Great."

That deflated my ego. So much for fame.

"He isn't from Soam, but he has been sent to bring us back into our land," another sheep explained.

"Drakkar The Great has conquered many armies and now will fight the Snardlins on our behalf," said Rosa.

"You must be careful if you are going to stay around here. The Snardlins patrol through here often," another sheep threw in.

"You are welcome to stay here at our camp if you like," another sheep offered joyfully. "We will prepare a great meal later. You are all invited."

We decided to camp for the night. The sheep were all so nice, considering what they had been through. They prepared a massive feast for us all, just as they promised. The food was mouthwatering. The desserts were delectable, and decadent. There were trays with pomegranates, olives, and figs. Some of the desserts were made of mint and dark chocolate. It was an incredible spread.

All the sheep, the loving animals that they were, seemed eager to please us as their guests. There seemed to be a hopeful spirit amongst them, despite the horrible situation they were in. I felt bad for them. I couldn't imagine being forced out of my own country.

While we sat and dined on the sheep's delicious food, I heard something fluttering behind me. I turned around to see what it was, but it flew out of the tent. I ran out of the tent to see what it was and saw an odd-looking small bird with a long beak.

"Extraordinary!" the bird exclaimed before taunting me. "You can't catch me! You can't catch me! Ha, ha, ha. You can't catch me."

"What is your name?" I asked.

"My name is Cece," said the bird. Cece reminded me of a toucan. His body was orange with a white stripe down his back. His beak was royal blue. "I'm telling King Arista that you are here. He will come and get you, ha, ha, ha!"

The bird was starting to irritate me with its constant ha, ha, ha-ing.

"If you can answer my riddle, I will not tell him you are here," Cece said. "But if you don't answer my riddle, I will tell the king."

This sounded like a trick, but I knew I had no choice but to try to answer the riddle. "Okay," I said. "Go ahead." I wasn't sure I was up to the challenge, but I was sure I didn't want some bird outsmarting me.

"As bark grows on a tree," Cece paused, "wherever your mind may be," he paused again, "if your mind starts to stray—"

Interrupting him, I completed the sentence, "let the gumdrops show you the way."

Cece looked stunned. His beak dropped to the ground, and he stammered, "but, but, but how … how did you know the riddle?"

"I just knew," I said, crossing my arms over my chest.

"Nobody has ever answered the riddle before," he said in a distressed voice. Then he turned blue all over.

I thought he might be sick. "Cece, are you alright?"

He wobbled back and forth and, in a weak voice, chortled, "Cece not feeling well." Then, after a little teeter, he fell over on his side. I ran to help him as his blueish hue grew darker.

"What can I do to help you?" I said nervously.

"Cece will be okay," he said weakly before standing to his feet. He walked around for a bit and sat by my side. I didn't understand what was happening. Was he well or not?

"Extraordinary!" exclaimed Cece.

"What's extraordinary?" I asked.

"I belong to you now," he said with a wink.

"What?"

"Yes, no one has ever figured out the riddle before, until now. You are Cece's master. Cece now your spy." His voice carried a strange enthusiasm for a bird who had just declared himself a servant to a girl like me.

"I don't want to be anyone's master, Cece."

"Too late now, Cece yours. Cece has spied on different clans for over a hundred years without a master. If anyone ever figured out Cece's riddle, Cece would then become theirs to help protect them. You figured it out. How can I be of service to you?"

"I will have to think about that one. Let's go back to the tent."

I walked back into the tent and Cece followed. When we entered, everyone fell silent. All eyes turned toward Cece. He began to shake and looked stressed.

"There's that traitor, kill him!" someone yelled.

I jumped in front of Cece, shouting, "Nobody's killing anybody! He is my spy now. I figured out the riddle." As I said it, I realized how silly it sounded. The crowd gasped.

"You figured out the riddle?" said a sheep called Nelah.

"Yes, I did. So, he belongs to me now. He will be of great help to us all," I said confidently. No one knew I was really trying to convince myself.

Everyone in the tent went back to what they had been doing before. A sheep came to me and said, "Tiffany, my name is Jordan."

"Hi there. It's nice to meet you, Jordan."

"We're glad you are here. We hope that you and your friends can help us get our homeland back."

"What happened to King Zirdak?" I asked.

"King Zirdak put a coalition together to overthrow King Arista and the Snardlin empire. He was unsuccessful. King Arista took King Zirdak into captivity and blinded him. We didn't hear much more about him after that, but King Arista burned Soam down and destroyed everything in it."

"You aren't the only ones left of Soam, are you?"

"No, there are more of us, but we are scattered. King Arista brought the important ones out first. The wealthy and well-to-do were held captive. The ones like us, who were not wealthy, were left here and there because we were not much of a threat."

"That explains all the nice jewelry and clothes and things," I said.

"Yes, those things were left behind," Jordan said with sadness. "The wise one warned King Zirdak not to attack the Snardlins. Then the wicked ones influenced him to go through with the rebellion. There were a couple of different waves of expulsion from Soam. We were the last."

"I'm so sorry," I said. "I feel terrible for you guys. I will help you anyway I can."

"With the help of Drakkar the Great and your army, I think we might have a chance at overthrowing the Snardlins."

It was encouraging for Jordan to think that we could help. But I did not feel confident in myself. I wasn't sure what we were up against, but I knew this would be more difficult than anything we had faced so far.

In short order, Vandy joined us. He looked me in the eye and said, "Tiffany, we need to come up with a plan to attack the Snardlins."

"We could get Cece to search out the Snardlin forces," I offered.

"Did somebody say 'Cece'?" the bird asked, landing on my shoulder.

"He sure is nosy," said Vandy.

I laughed. "Maybe that's why he is a spy."

Vandy snickered as Cece gave him a cold stare. Then Vandy said, "That is a wonderful idea. Cece could scout the area and give us an idea of the Snardlin forces' movements."

"I could go with Cece and get a closer look at their activities," Britny said.

"Brilliant!" exclaimed Vandy.

"Extraordinary!" said Cece.

Cece and Britny set off on their recon mission while Vandy and I gathered our troops and delegated tasks for each one to complete. Everyone seemed to be ready to help the citizens of Soam when the time came.

Strider wrote a list of things needed to build weapons. A couple of the Soamites gathered the items on the list and gave them to the Strider. The Hakkamadoos immediately began building weapons. Another Soamite pulled out a map of where they had hidden weaponry many years ago. The Soamites were not typical fighters, but they realized they must regain their homeland. It was their primary purpose now.

"How many troops does King Arista have?" Alanis asked.

"Thousands," Rosa said.

"Thousands!" exclaimed Harlow.

"When we left Soam, the Snardlins had hundreds of troops," said Alanis.

"A lot can happen in fifty years," said one of the Hakkamadoos.

I suddenly felt tired. I asked one of the Soamites if I could sleep on one of their cots.

"Of course, you can, dear," she said reassuringly.

I lay on a cot and pondered what the next day might bring. As I did, I fell asleep. I slept until right before daybreak when I heard someone moving about. Stepping out of the tent, I saw everyone gathered in groups. Each group focused on different tasks related to building a fighting force.

Vandy, Harlow, and Britny were in a circle with some of the Hakkamadoos studying a map. Strider was in a class with Rosa and the rest of the Hakkamadoos building weapons. Alanis, Jordan, and some Soamites examined some weapons the Snardlins had left behind during the Soamite diaspora. They were huge and heavy. Seeing the weapons gave everyone an idea of how strong those creatures were.

Through the corner of my eye, I caught a glimpse of a light several hundred yards away, in the forest. It quickly disappeared. Then I saw it again. It appeared like light reflecting from a mirror. Then I saw a figure walking into the forest.

I grabbed my slingshot and ran toward the forest where I saw the figure. It was quite a distance through the muggy darkness. When I got to the forest, I saw no one there. The deeper into the forest I walked, the darker it became and the staler the air became. I grew nervous, and anxious.

I felt like something might be following me. I looked to the right and no one was there. I looked left and nothing was there either. So, I spun around. I grew so nervous I decided to load my slingshot.

"Hey, kid!" said a voice.

I dropped my slingshot and screamed at the top of my lungs. In the darkness of the forest, I could make out a vague shadow of a form that looked familiar to me. The figure stepped forward and I knelt to pick up my slingshot. Careful not to take my eyes off the figure, I felt around in the dark until my fingers touched it. I slipped my fingers under it and gripped it tight. Through a glint of moonlight pressing through the trees, I caught a glimpse of a familiar face.

"Englow! How did you get here?"

"Well, I know a little bit about windows of time myself," he said proudly. I embraced him and hugged him as hard as I could, grasping my slingshot tight in my hands.

"It's so good to see you. Why are you here?" I asked through tears.

"Do you remember the walls in my lair, Tiffany? Do you remember how you could see events as you passed through the halls?"

"Yes, Englow. I remember."

"I saw something disturbing. You and the Misfits will be betrayed," he said.

My heart dropped. *Who could it be,* I thought? Everyone around us seems so nice. It didn't make sense.

"You have heard the phrase, 'Luna Toosa'?" Englow asked.

"Yes."

"Luna Toosa is what the Snardlins call the gumdrops. They want to use the power of the gumdrops to do something evil. The gumdrops are one part of what they need to complete the formula for a power more destructive than anything in history."

"How do we stop them?" I asked.

"Tiffany, that is something you will have to figure out. You are the only one who has ever been able to control the gumdrops. I only know what they can do. I do not know how you can use their power."

A lot of things were going through my mind. I tried to think of what the gumdrops' power could be. My mind jumped to the coming betrayal. *Who could betray us,* I wondered. *Is someone here sympathetic to the Snardlins? Does someone just want the power to destroy us all? How could I fight side-by-side with them not knowing if they were going to betray me?* I suddenly became suspicious of everyone.

Cece and Britny returned from their mission and hooked up with Englow and me in the forest.

"Extraordinary!" yelled Cece.

"You scared me to death! How did you know we were out here, Cece?" I asked.

"Cece knows everything."

"Cece knows everything because he is nosy," said Britny.

"Hello, Britny," said Englow.

"I'm happy to see you, Englow," Britny said syrupy.

Cece fluttered in front of Englow, bouncing in midair like a balloon on a string. "I'm Cece. It is an extraordinary pleasure to meet you, Englow."

"Nice to meet you, too, Cece."

"We scouted the land, but we could not find the Snardlins," said Britny.

"I think they have gone back to the main city," said Cece.

"We will go out and scout again later. We are both tired from flying all night," Britny added, landing on my shoulder.

"I must go now," said Englow.

"Why do you have to leave?" I asked.

"There's no one to collect the fees for entering Emerald Mountain," he said.

We both laughed. Britny chuckled and flew off with Cece toward the tents.

"In all seriousness, I must go, but remember everything you have learned, and remember what I have told you," Englow said wrapping his arms around me. After a long hug, he disappeared into the forest, and the forest fell silent again.

10 BUILDING THE COALITION

On my way back to the village, when I reached the edge of the forest, I caught sight of a huge army surrounding the village. *That can't be good*, I thought. Startled and fearful, I ran as fast as I could toward the village hoping I wasn't too late. Inside the village, I saw Velvet, Ronin, and Harlow sitting. They looked intense, as if their attention was focused on some drama before their eyes. I loaded a gumdrop into my slingshot and cautiously walked toward them. Velvet and Ronin began shaking their heads from side to side. It looked as if they were telling me "No," but if they were in danger, then I had to try to save them.

In front of them, with his back toward me, stood a man with long blonde hair. His hair was longer and blonder than mine, and that's saying something!

He wasn't a real big man, but he exuded a confidence like no one I've ever seen. I approached him with my slingshot loaded, trying to get as close as I could to determine how threatening he truly was. One of his soldiers spotted me, picked up his bow, and loaded an arrow. "Stop right there," I shouted, "or Blondie gets it!" I made sure to aim my weapon at the blonde man's head. The crowd stepped back in awe and began shaking their heads in the same manner as Ronin and Velvet. "I do not fear these people! I'm a warrior and I'm going to take care of them right now!"

I didn't believe what I was saying, but I knew I had to make it sound believable.

The blonde-haired man turned to look at me. "Young lady, what is your name?" he asked. His voice carried an ironic gentleness with it.

"My name is Tiffany Triumph," I said proudly.

"And my name is Drakkar."

I nearly swallowed my tongue. I couldn't believe I almost shot the king that was here to help restore Soam. The whole crowd looked at me in silence, and I was so embarrassed I could feel my face turn red.

"Um, I'm so sorry. I thought you were here to attack us."

"No, just here to help." Drakkar smiled.

Velvet sauntered up beside me and whispered, "We tried to tell you."

Before I could respond, Drakkar stepped forward and began to speak with all the confidence of a trained warrior. "We have a monumental task ahead of us," he said. "We must be strong and courageous. We must work together to defeat the Snardlins."

Strider stepped up on a huge boulder and shouted, "Our allegiance is to Soam and its citizens. We Hakkamadoos left our home because of the Snardlins. Now, we will fight to help the Soamites get their home back. Drakkar, you have our full commitment and allegiance to help you conquer Snard."

Vandy stood, beaming with pride. "Soam has a special place in the Misfits' hearts, as well. We will fight in honor of King Zirdak. It will be our privilege to fight alongside you, Drakkar!"

Drakkar, mounting his horse, said, "My army must first conquer the Orlot and the Janus tribes. Be prepared to fight. We will return soon." The crowd cheered as Drakkar and his army bounded east out of the village, fast as lightning. The Soamites and the rest of the crew went back to building shields and weapons.

When the excitement wore down, Vandy asked me, "What do you think, Tiffany? Do we have a chance?"

"It looks like Drakkar the Great has a big enough army," I said. "He seems confident. So, yes, I think we have a chance at beating the Snardlins."

After agreeing, he pondered for a moment, then added, "We must work on our strategy. We will have many fighters, but the Snardlins are big creatures and dwarf all of us."

"We must outwit the Snardlins," said Strider pacing back and forth.

"Velvet, Alanis, and I can entice the Snardlins to chase us," said Ronin, scurrying around the camp.

Velvet rolled her eyes. "That may be the dumbest thing you've ever said, Ronin. How is having the Snardlins chase us going to help win the battle?"

"Quit being so cruel, Velvet. Ronin is trying to help," Alanis pled.

"Are you guys thinking what I'm thinking?" I asked. Both Strider and Vandy grinned at me. "That's it! Ronin, you are brilliant!" I shouted.

"I am?" Ronin sounded confused before coming to her senses. "Oh, yes, I am," he beamed.

"Yes, you are we'll use the Snardlin's huge size to their disadvantage. They are big and strong, but they may tire easily because of their size," said Strider.

"I suggest we don't begin with hand-to-hand combat. We give the Snardlins a little run around to drain their strength. Then, when they get tired, we attack with vengeance." Vandy stressed *vengeance* as he thrust an air sword toward an invisible opponent.

"We will use this strategy when we can," Strider added, still pacing. "There will be times when we can't. In those times, we'll watch out for each other and make sure that none of us are outnumbered."

"We can have them chase us around when the time is right," said Harlow.

"Just don't get caught," said Velvet.

"Velvet and Ronin, you are not going into battle," I said gently. "But I do think we have a good strategy. I'm sure Drakkar will have a plan to follow, but we will use this strategy once we get into the battle."

With that, I went into the tent and checked my weapons. Then I inspected my pouch of gumdrops. I had more than I started with. They had multiplied, but how? I also noticed their colors were brighter. What power did the gumdrops have that made the Snardlins want them so badly, I wondered. Would I be able to harness that power? Could I gain the power before going into battle? I had so many questions and so few answers.

"Extraordinary," said Cece.

"I thought you were resting," I said.

"I rested." After a pause, he added, "Ooh, pretty, pretty, pretty. What are those?" As soon as he saw the gumdrops, his feathers turned black.

"*Those* are none of your business." I casually slid the gumdrops back into the pouch. Cece continued to focus on the pouch until I dropped it into my shirt pocket and walked out of the tent.

We worked until nightfall, had a feast, and went to bed early. I slept hard. At home, I'm a big fan of sleeping.

In the middle of the night, I heard some shuffling. I rose from my cot and caught Cece with my gumdrop pouch in his grubby little hands. He gazed at the myriad-colored light emanating from them. I snatched the pouch out of his hands and yelled, "No!"

Cece's eyes glossed over and grew bigger. He lifted himself off the ground and mumbled, "Luna Toosa."

I punched him in the beak and watched as he fell to the ground.

After lifting himself up, he asked, "Tiffany, why did you punch Cece?"

"You were acting strange. You got into my gumdrops and acted evilly. You called them 'Luna Toosa'."

"Luna what?"

It was obvious that Cece didn't realize what had just happened. There was a power with the gumdrops, but even more power when evil was involved.

"Cece sorry," he said as his face saddened.

"Stay out of my things," I said, picking up my pouch of gumdrops and shoving them under my pillow.

I awoke early the next morning. Only a few Hakkamadoos were awake. I walked around the camp and noted the progress everyone had made building the arsenal. When Strider saw me, he said, "Tiffany, something isn't right. I can sense it."

"What do you mean?"

"There is something in the air, and it feels evil."

Harlow sniffed the ground and agreed. I could feel it also but couldn't make out what it was.

About that time, Cece flew over with an invitation. "Come with Cece to the river. See if we can find sharp rocks for making spears."

"Okay," I said, and we traipsed off together toward the river.

The wind picked up. Something told me to turn around and go back to camp, but we continued to the river anyway. As soon as we made it to the riverbank, Cece started acting strangely again. He seemed nervous.

"Cece, what's the matter?" I asked. I heard some rustling in the trees, then a Snardlin jumped out of a tree onto the ground behind me.

Cece, with a look of satisfaction, pronounced, "I told you Cece could bring her to you."

"You betrayed me, Cece. How could you? I thought you were bound to me for life!"

"Not anymore. You have the Luna Toosa," he said.

Cece circled around behind me and snatched my pouch with the gumdrops in it. He flew to a Snardlin and dropped the pouch in its hands, then he flew away. The Snardlin opened the pouch. His eyes lit up like the creatures at Black Mountain as he fell into a trance. He seemed to be seeing things that I couldn't see when I touched the gumdrops, and he chanted, "Luna Toosa, Luna Toosa, Luna Toosa."

I didn't know what that meant, but I knew it wasn't good.

Demonic sounds rose from the river. They were high-pitch squeals as if someone was in agony. Then I heard crying followed my screaming, mixed with eerie voices shouting, "Let us out!" The disturbing sounds gave me cold chills all over my body.

The Snardlin grabbed the gumdrops one by one. Six of them. Then I remembered what Englow had told me about not holding more than six gumdrops at once. I ran as fast as I could in the opposite direction from the Snardlin, and just when I thought I was in the clear, I heard an explosion and felt the subsequent shockwave. The force of the explosion blew me off my feet.

The next thing I heard was Britny's voice. "Tiffany, can you hear me?"

I could hear her, but her voice was muffled by the ringing in my ears. I fell in and out of consciousness. Then my eyes opened wide, and I could see several figures standing above me.

"Are you alright?" asked Alanis.

Vandy asked, "Are you okay, Tiffany?"

Harlow licked my face. Velvet and Ronin nudged me with their noses. Strider said, "Let's help her up."

After they helped me to my feet, I stumbled a bit and had a terrible headache. My body ached all over.

As my vision improved, I could see trees broken and burnt leaves of ash falling to the ground. I could smell charred wood. It looked as if someone had built a bonfire that got out of control. I looked around and could not believe the devastation the explosion had caused. I was fortunate to be alive. A greater power must have been looking out for me.

I walked around a bit and reached for my pouch. It was gone. Something strange happened next. The gumdrops began to roll across the ground toward me, coming from every every direction. I saw them coming out from under bushes, and from underneath logs. I saw one pop out of a hole in the ground about the size of what a rabbit might dig. It was as if the gumdrops had hidden until I woke up and gathered my senses. Then they started coming my way, stopping at my feet. Strider, throwing his pouch toward me, said, "Here, use my pouch."

Once Strider's pouch was in my possession, the gumdrops jumped into it on their own, as if some magnetic force had drawn them.

"What happened, Tiffany?" Britny asked.

"I don't know. I remember an explosion, but I don't know what happened before that."

I could not remember. I had the same feeling two years earlier when I hit my head on a balance beam during gymnastics practice. As my head cleared, we left the river and headed back to camp. Velvet and Ronin must have thought they had lost me for good. Everywhere I went, they were right behind me.

When we reached the camp, Rosa approached me and said, "Here, my dear, drink this pomegranate juice. It will help with the swelling."

I drank it as I sat in the tent, struggling to remember anything before the explosion. My head still ached. Things were a bit fuzzy.

"Where's Cece?" asked Britny.

Where was Cece? I remembered going to the river and—"That's it!" I said. "It was Cece who led me to the Snardlin."

"I told you not to trust him," said one of the Soamites.

"Cece betrayed me," I said, still finding it hard to believe.

"The Snardlins know we are here now. It's only a matter of time before they come to attack us," said Vandy.

"The land of Snard is east of here. Travel time is a few days. You must start right away so you can attack them before they come here," said Rosa.

"We have to find Drakkar first, because we won't have a chance of defeating the Snardlins without his army," said Harlow.

"I will locate Drakkar," said Britny, and she flew east with all the speed and agility of a locust.

The Hakkamadoos practiced fighting one another. I went out to practice my shooting skills. I found myself in the desert shooting at vultures when I saw a herd of Ibecks running across the plains. They seemed to be running scared. I understood that completely. I felt like running scared myself. I was a twelve-year-old girl who had never seen a battlefield. I did not have the confidence in myself to take on such a task. How would I do? How would any of us do going against such an empire? I knew those questions would be answered soon. Then I heard a voice.

The voice said, "Tiffany."

"Yes, Counselor," I said.

"Do not be afraid," he said. "You will not be alone. I will be there for you. Whether in battle or everyday life, I will never put you in a situation that you cannot handle. You will know when the day of battle shall begin. Look for the red skies in the morning. Red skies in the morning indicate bad weather in the evening, which will be to your advantage."

"So, we should fight during a storm? How will that be to our advantage?" No answer. "Counselor, are you there?"

And just like that, he was gone.

I practiced for several more hours before nightfall. I thought about what the Counselor had told me. The fear went away. There was a warm feeling of protection that I could not explain. My confidence was high knowing that the Counselor promised me he would be there with me during the battle. There is no better feeling than knowing someone is there for you, no matter what you are going through.

I headed back to camp, scanning the skies. I had an awesome sense of peace that I had not felt since the first time the Counselor had spoken to me. Sometimes I may not think the Counselor is there because I do not hear Him. But He is there. I can feel His presence.

11 THE JOURNEY FOR FREEDOM

"It has been days since we've seen Britny. Where is she?" asked Alanis.

"I hope she's okay," said Harlow.

I walked out of the tent and noticed it was hotter than normal. At the high point of summer, there wasn't as much wind as we were used to. That made the heat unbearable.

We would be crossing the desert soon and didn't have horses, unlike Drakkar and his army. That meant we'd have to walk the whole journey. I wondered if we would survive the trek across the barren desert, much less the fight against the Snardlin empire. Rosa said it was over eight hundred miles to Snard. I guessed it would take weeks, maybe months, to get there. Would we be fit to fight after walking that far through the desert?

I decided I would train while waiting for Britny and Drakkar to return. I trained in the heat to get my body adjusted to the desert climate. To further condition my body, I ran around the camp daily. I had trained rigorously for gymnastics, but not as hard as I was training for battle. After several days, I could run five miles in the heat. There were times when I felt that I would pass out, but I didn't quit despite sweating so much. I could tell I had lost weight but had gained muscle mass. At night, I ate a lot of protein and drank as much water as possible.

I found a tree in the woods that had been broken by the wind. A couple of the Hakkamadoos helped me tear the branches off to make a meg shift balance beam. I practiced on it for hours, holding handstands until my strength was all gone. I also practiced jumps, cartwheels, and spins. It made me stronger, and my muscles more toned. In the afternoon, I climbed lebanon trees. They were some of the mightiest trees I've ever seen. I've always been afraid of heights, but I pushed myself to climb as high as I could for the sake of being ready for the looming fight.

The Hakkamadoos practiced fighting with me. They were strong and nimble. They had made their own protection shields, which they would use to deflect stones I shot at them with my slingshot.

I grew so fond of the Hakkamadoos. Their body language told me they missed their homeland. Strider said I should learn to Charan, which is a Hakkamadoo word for wrestling. He told me I needed to use my small frame and strength to attack the Snardlin legs, if I got into a situation where I couldn't use my weapon.

Practice also included grappling with one of the Hakkamadoos. She was very strong and pinned me in a matter of seconds. But I went back to her again. That time, she pinned me even faster. That angered me, so I went after her hard. She spun me onto my stomach and accidentally busted my nose on the ground. When she expressed sympathy, I took advantage of the opportunity to stand up and take her legs out from under her. She hit the ground hard. I pounced on her and pinned her.

"Good job! You are learning fast," she said. After a little more practice, we headed back to camp.

"Tiffany, wait up for me." Britny's voice came from behind. I turned around and saw her flying toward me. She landed on my shoulder and said, "I made it back."

"I'm so glad you're back. We haven't seen you for several days now. We were all worried." I genuinely felt relieved.

"I flew for miles before I caught up with Drakkar and his army," she said between pants. "I got caught up in a bad sandstorm and lost my way for a few days on my way back here."

"Did you tell Drakkar about the Snardlins knowing our whereabouts and that we need to attack them as soon as possible?"

"Yes, he said that his army would wait, if they could, until you and the Hakkamadoos got there."

"The only problem with that is we have to travel on foot. There's no way we can get there in time," I said. As I spoke, everyone looked toward the sky.

The ground darkened with shadows from above. I looked up and saw the albatrosses coming in for a landing.

"Hi, Tiffany!" exclaimed Abby.

"Hi, Abby!" I yelled gleefully.

The albatrosses landed. The Hakkamadoos and the Misfits ran out to greet them.

"What are you guys doing here?" asked Alanis.

"I brought them here," said Britny proudly.

"No wonder you were gone so long," said Vandy.

"We heard you needed some transport," said Abby.

"But Abby, you are seabirds," I argued. "We need to go hundreds of miles in the desert. It will be strenuous for you."

"We will fly at night and rest in caves during the day," she said. "Whenever we see freshwater, we will stop. All of you should bring plenty of water in case it is scarce. Get packed at once. The sun is about to go down. We must leave soon so that we can get as much flight time in as possible before daybreak."

Vandy shouted, "Load up your belongings! Bring plenty of water! We leave at once!"

We gathered our weapons and supplies, then we loaded them on the albatrosses' backs. Velvet, Ronin, and I loaded up on Abby. The Soamites thanked us for our assistance, and we were off.

The albatrosses flew in a single file pattern. We climbed higher and higher until the air became cooler. The moon guided our way. I looked at the stars and wondered what was beyond. The constellations were so bright and close I felt like I could touch them.

"If you would like to sleep, Tiffany," Abby yelled over her left wing, "tie a rope around some of my feathers on my back. Tie the other end around your waist and you won't fall off. You can sleep. Me and the other albatrosses will take turns sleeping during flight to keep watch out for any danger."

I did as Abby suggested and strapped Velvet and Ronin in first. Then I tethered myself to the bird and fell asleep.

"Wake up, Tiffany." Abby's voice pulled me out of a deep sleep to the break of daylight. Ahead of us was the most beautiful rainbow I had ever seen. The colors were so vibrant they reflected the sky like a mirror. I felt like I could touch the rainbow as we went through it. Behind me, Vandy looked as amazed as I was.

The albatrosses flew faster. We climbed high into the sky, into the rainbow. Then we dove. Straight down. We moved so fast Velvet and Ronin latched onto my clothes, fearing they would fall off. The albatrosses aligned themselves into a straight line again.

"We must stop and rest for the day," Abby said.

We landed near some caves in the desert and unloaded the albatrosses as they drank water. Then we ate some fish the Soamites had broiled.

"Let's go to the caves to escape the heat, and to rest," Abby suggested.

We found caves to store our belongings in. The caves were so much cooler than the desert sun. The Hakkamadoos did not like the heat much, so they stayed inside their caves during the day. I slept all night and was fully rested by morning. I decided to go exploring. Vandy and Britny joined me.

Before we left the desert where the Soamites were camped, Rosa had told us that many of the Soamites had been exiled to an area where their ancestors had been enslaved for several hundred years. What an awful way to live. These people had been forced to leave their home country. They had no ruler, no government, and little hope of returning to their homeland. The Snardlins had destroyed their lives and seemed to hate everything about the Soamites. I wondered why. Was there a legitimate reason, or was it plain evil?

"Britny, how much farther do we have to travel?"

"We are not quite halfway, Tiffany. It took the Soamites five months to travel back to Trav on foot when returning from their exile."

"Are they somewhere in Trav?" I asked. "The short amount of time we were in Trav was not a good experience."

"Yes, Trav is a hideous place," Vandy said. "That just shows how bad it got in Soam for the Soamites to return to Trav."

"When we left Soam, there were rumors of the Snardlins coming to take the land, but they had not invaded yet," said Britny.

"It was shocking to see what had transpired since we left," said Vandy.

As we explored our surroundings, the sky turned pitch black, and I noticed the air getting cooler.

"What is happening?" Vandy asked.

"A storm, I guess," said Britny. But I knew what was going on. I had experienced it before. Then I saw the Black Mountain queen in the distance. The desert sand turned black and smooth like glass.

Between us and the queen was a walkway. She was at least a football field away from us. The walkway was narrow and long, reminding me of a black marble floor. Before I could blink, the queen was right in front of me. She was one of the most beautiful women I had ever seen. Flawless in every sense of the word. Orianthia, the beautiful queen of Black Mountain.

"Tiffany, I can hand you a victory over the Snardlin empire." The queen spoke in a velvet voice, smooth and convincing. "I can make you the most loved and admired person in the world. Would you like to be an Olympic gold medalist? I can do that for you. I can transfer to you my own beauty. I can give you all that you desire." Her elegance was striking, her voice hypnotizing. "All you must do is come with me. I will give you all the power and prestige in the world. You have nothing to lose and everything to gain."

I couldn't move. I had fallen into a trance.

"Tiffany, remember what the Counselor told you." Vandy's voice massaged my ears, reminding me of who I was and who I was to serve.

"Do not say that name!" shouted Orianthia.

"The Counselor is with you always!" shouted Britny.

"Stop saying that name!" the queen shouted again. She thrust her hand toward Vandy and knocked him off his feet. He fell and she hadn't even touched him.

Britny flew behind me and whispered into my ear, "Do not give in to temptation, Tiffany. You are stronger than that."

I noticed the queen's face changing. She was losing her beauty. Her elegance fading. Her eyes went from alluring to scary.

"The Counselor will defeat you!" Vandy exclaimed.

The queen screamed that high pitch shrill that I heard before and said, "You cannot resist me forever, Tiffany. You will be weak soon. I will control you then!"

The sky exploded with lightning and thunder and Orianthia appeared instantly at the other end of the black glass walkway. Then she disappeared. The walkway rolled up like a scroll and vanished. The sun returned, the air became warm again, and everything went back to the way it was before the queen arrived.

"I felt her power drawing me in," I said shamefully.

"Orianthia can draw anyone in. We all have weak moments. Always look for the Counselor for strength," said Britny.

"I have felt her power before, but that was the strongest it's ever been," Vandy said, back on his feet.

We returned to the caves. The day was almost over, and I was getting hungry and tired. Everyone had a meal and relaxed for a while. The albatrosses were still sleeping. I did not wake them because I knew they needed as much rest as they could get. We would be leaving later in the night. Still, I went to sleep for a while.

I dreamed about the place where the butterflies were, again. I dreamed about Gem and how sweet she was. She made me very comfortable. I cannot explain why, but she did.

Abby woke me later and said, "Tiffany, we should go now. If we fly all night, I think we can make it to Snard by mid-morning." We gathered our supplies and weapons and loaded them onto the albatrosses. One by one, we took off into the moonlit sky.

The albatrosses flew faster than ever. The air was cool and crisp. I could feel the strength in Abby's wings. Those birds thrived off the clean night air.

As we flew, I thought of how close we were to a confrontation with the Snardlins. Reality started to set in. I felt anxious that the biggest moment of my life was just around the corner.

12 THE MIGHTY TEN THOUSAND

"There's Drakkar the Great and his army!" shouted Harlow.

It was daytime now. We had flown all night. The albatrosses flew fast. I did not expect to arrive at Snard so quickly.

"What an army!" shouted Alanis.

What an army indeed. There must have been ten thousand soldiers. I saw hundreds of chariots. The sun glittered off their shiny spears and swords. I could see men carrying battle rams. Some of the soldiers wore metal suits.

We landed outside Drakkar's camp and unloaded the albatrosses. I walked to the camp and saw a mighty battalion of fighters standing in formation. Everyone was fit and ready for battle. I did not see Drakkar right away, but several of his soldiers greeted me. I walked to one of the chariots to get a firsthand look at its design.

"Get out of my chariot!" said a tiny voice from inside.

I looked around but couldn't see anyone. "I'm sorry," I said. "I did not mean to intrude. Um, where are you?"

"Down here!" the soldier shouted, shaking his fist.

I looked down and saw a guinea pig.

"Hi there! I'm Tiffany," I said joyfully.

"You are on my chariot, Tiffany. Get off now!"

Drakkar walked up and perched himself on the opposite side of the chariot. "So, this is your chariot, Boris?"

Boris looked at me with fear in his eyes. I could hear him gulp. "Uh, well, you see, um."

"I'm sorry. I did not mean to cause a problem," I said.

"No, no, not a problem at all. You must learn how the chariot works. Soon you will be riding your own," said Drakkar.

"She will be what?" shouted Boris.

"Tiffany and her army are here to help fight the Snardlins," said Drakkar.

"We don't need any help. We have the strongest army in the world," Boris bragged.

About that time, Vandy joined us. "We were chosen to help fight the Snardlins," he said proudly, "and that's what we intend to do, you little varmint."

As he spoke, Vandy jumped upon a nearby table. Boris jumped onto the other side. "Don't you dare call me a varmint, desert rat!"

Vandy and Boris argued over the prominence of their species for several minutes. When I'd had enough, I said, "Come on, guys. Enough already." Then I heard a loud Wop!

Drakkar had stuck his sword into the wooden table, right between Boris and Vandy. He looked irritated. Vandy and Boris shook themselves off and put on ridiculous smiles showing off all their teeth. They looked frightened.

"Stop the arguing at once! We have an enemy to defeat! You're wasting time and energy!" shouted Drakkar. Vandy and Boris suddenly quietened as Drakkar turned to me. "Check out all the fighting equipment and get familiar with it, Tiffany. I have to meet with my commanders and finish working on the battle plan."

I walked to the archery equipment and picked up one of the bows. I shot a few arrows with it but kept missing the targets. A couple of the younger soldiers laughed at me. One of them shot an arrow with his own bow and hit the center of the target. Another soldier's arrow landed in the center of the target right next to the first. They celebrated and laughed at me.

As they turned to walk off, I pulled out my slingshot, took an arrowhead from one of the Drakkar soldiers' quiver, and loaded it into my slingshot. I pulled the sling back as hard as I ever had. It sparkled and emitted a bright light. When I released the arrow, it flew so fast I could hear it whistle. It slid between both soldiers' arrows and knocked them off the target. The soldiers turned their heads to look. I winked at them. At that, I left the two of them standing there gawking at each other and couldn't help but giggle as I strolled away.

"Tiffany," Vandy said as he approached. "Where is everybody? I don't see the Hakkamadoos or the rest of the Misfits."

"I don't know. Let's go find them."

We went to the spot where we landed and saw that the albatrosses were preparing to leave. "Tiffany," Abby said, "we are going to fly to those caves on the cliff a few miles back. We are going to get some rest before heading home."

"We are so grateful to you and the rest of the albatrosses, Abby. We couldn't have made it here without you." I was so sad to see them go I teared up.

"You are welcome, Tiffany. We were glad to be able to help."

"Will I ever see you again, Abby?"

"I don't know. But something tells me that, somehow, we will cross paths," she said, smiling. With that, Abby and the albatrosses disappeared into the desert sky.

Harlow raced over and, huffing and puffing, said, "Tiffany, I have orders from Drakkar for us to go on a scouting mission to the city of Snard. We must leave at once."

"Okay," I said. "Then let's go."

Before we could leave, the Misfits, Velvet, and Ronin approached us.

"I want to go too!" said Alanis.

Britny said, "I'm in!"

Velvet and Ronin both jumped on my shoulders. "Okay," I giggled, "so we're all going."

We loaded some horses with food and water and checked our weapons.

About that time, Strider walked up and asked, "Where are you going?"

Harlow said proudly, "We are going on a scouting mission to Snard."

"Do you mind if some of us Hakkamadoos tag along?" said Strider.

"Absolutely, you can go!" I said happily.

"We don't need everyone in the camp to go on this mission," whispered Vandy.

"Not everyone in the camp is going, just a few of us," I whispered back. Then I turned and saw fifty Hakkamadoos behind me, ready to go. "It's still not everyone," I said with a grin. "We will be better off with more fighters, in case there is some trouble."

"Whatever, but if these Hakkamadoos get us caught, it is your fault," whispered Vandy sarcastically.

Velvet, Ronin, and I filed into a chariot. Everyone else got in line behind us, and we headed east.

"Wait, wait for me! Drakkar said I should go with you!" shouted Boris, running after us.

"That's just great," said Vandy with a scowl. "We get to ride with that little rodent carrying a big attitude."

"Hush. He might hear you," I said, stopping the chariot and letting Boris jump in. Velvet and Ronin licked their chops. "Don't you even think about it, you two!"

The cats walked to the back of the chariot and lay down. Boris had the cutest little armored suit on with a mask that covered his face. He jumped on the front of the chariot and yelled, "To Snard we march!"

"Good grief," Velvet said with a sneer.

The chariots were incredibly fast. They were heavy, very dense, and strong. Each was pulled by four powerful horses. Nisean horses, very robust, led some of them. Bigger than average horses, Niseans look like war horses. Most of them are white with black, flowing manes and braided tails. I could sense an intense power emanating from them.

We moved steadily for a few hours before stopping to water the horses and rest. It was late afternoon, and the heat of the sun was fading. I asked

Boris how much farther it was to Snard. "About three more hours," he said. We decided to make a camp since the sun would be setting soon.

We built a fire and one of the Hakkamadoos prepared dinner. I could smell the aromas of roasted vegetables and baked bread in the air. We had a wonderful meal and enjoyed conversation around the campfire.

The Hakkamadoos took turns watching for the enemy during the night. I felt more at ease knowing that Strider and his forces were there to protect us.

"Let's look at the map," said Vandy.

We sat and studied the map Drakkar had given Vandy before we left. "We are here," Boris pointed to a spot on the map. "These lines that you see drawn by the river are trenches Drakkar is digging to drain the river."

"Why would he want to do that?" I asked.

"The river goes right through the middle of town. Drakkar's plan is to drain the river low enough and march through the riverbed into town. That will make for a great attack point," Boris said.

"That's a good plan," said Vandy.

"Indeed," I said. "The city is a fortress. It is almost impossible to attack from the gates. There are Snardlins everywhere."

Everyone besides the couple of Hakkamadoos taking first watch turned in for the night. The desert was hot during the day but cold at night. I put a blanket on the ground near the warm fire. Ronin and Velvet lay down on the blanket with me. We stared at the luminous stars in the night sky until falling asleep.

The next morning, we got up early and loaded the horses. The weather was pleasant, and the desert hadn't started to get hot yet. We headed east, riding fast through the desert sand. We traveled for a few hours until we came to a body of water.

"There's the gulf," said Boris. "We will follow the gulf north until we see the city of Snard. We came the long way around so we wouldn't be spotted by the Snardlins."

After a short break, we headed north. A couple of hours later, we could see Snard. It was a magnificent city. The walls were tall and menacing. There were gigantic towers all around the city. But the most awesome thing was the gate at the entrance. It was so tall it seemed no one would ever be able to scale it. There were animal drawings across the front of the gate, each etched in gold. Dragons, lions, and some other animals I did not recognize.

The most beautiful thing I saw were the brilliant blue bricks that composed the gate. The bricks appeared as if they had a shiny glaze on them. It was hard to believe something so beautiful harbored something so evil inside.

We could see the Snardlins encamped around the front of the city. They were expecting Drakkar at any moment. Boris said, "We must get word back to Drakkar and let him know the Snardlins are preparing for him. We must do this before they send out spies to look for us."

"I will go," said Britny.

"Be careful," said Alanis.

Britny flew fast to give our report to Drakkar. We returned to the coastline until Drakkar and his army arrived. There, we found an area where we could hide. It's not exactly easy to hide a crowd, but we did it.

All we could do was wait. We ate some dried foods and slept for the night as we waited for Britny to return with Drakkar and his army.

The seabirds woke me by calling to each other. The Hakkamadoos were spearing fish down at the shoreline. Vandy broiled fish over a beach fire. Boris helped him and, of course, they argued constantly. Ronin and Velvet chased sand crabs on the beach and had a good time doing it. Harlow sniffed around at the seashells. Alanis perched on a rock and watched everyone.

I wondered if this would be the last time we would all be together and happy. My heart sank as I thought this might be the last time I'd see Velvet and Ronin. I love those two cats, and the many different characters I've met along the way. I grew so fond of the Misfits, I felt responsible for them. I thought I was not going to let them down. More importantly, I could not let the Counselor down. War was eminent. I was prepared, and I knew that we would win with the guidance of The Counselor.

We continued to practice fighting and maneuvering while waiting for Drakkar to join us for battle. Boris filled all of us in on the details of the city. He made a make-shift model of Snard out of sand on the beach. The rest of us studied the model so we'd be familiar with the layout of the city.

Boris gathered seashells and put them in areas on the model to represent where the guards would be protecting the fortress. I studied these areas to give me an idea when to use my slingshot and the gumdrops. I would have to make sure the gumdrops were not seen. The Snardlins could not get their hands on them. If they did, it would be catastrophic.

"Is that thunder?" asked Ronin.

"I don't know," said Harlow.

"Drakkar!" exclaimed Boris.

We ran to the top of the cliff and saw Drakkar the Great and his mighty army. The army looked as if it covered the entire desert. The noise from the horses and chariots did sound like thunder. Britny landed on my shoulder and shouted, "We're here!"

The mightiest army in the world had just shown up. It was time for us to show up and fight.

13 RED SKIES

"Here comes Drakkar," said Strider.

Drakkar headed our way with several of his men. We went to greet them. "Hello," he said. After we returned the greeting, Drakkar got straight to business. "We will attack tomorrow at noon," he said.

One of Drakkar's commanders pulled out a map of the battle plan as Drakkar continued to talk. "We will get everyone in their positions in the morning. We intend to attack the front of the city first. Once we back the Snardlins into their city, Tiffany, I will signal for you and your to troops enter through the riverbed, which we have been slowly draining. I will send five thousand troops to go with you. I will lead the other five thousand troops from outside the city walls. Be watchful of the towers. The Snardlins will attack from those points."

After his brief, Drakkar rode off. I was stunned. He wanted me to lead a brigade of more than five thousand into battle. Was he crazy? I almost panicked. I'm not a leader of an army. I grew more nervous.

"Are you all right, Tiffany?" Britny asked.

"No," I said.

"I know you are worried about what you are about to face, and you have a right to be concerned. But we all have the upmost confidence in you, Tiffany."

"I know that it is my responsibility to do what the Counselor asks of me. I have trained for battle and worked on building my confidence. But I don't know if I will ever have the confidence to do what Drakkar has asked me to do." I released my frustrations with fast talk. "Where is the Counselor? Why isn't he here to reassure me? Sometimes I wonder if he hears me when I speak to him."

"Tiffany, the Counselor is always there. Sometimes we may not think that He is listening, but he is. We should trust him," Britny said encouragingly.

I knew she was right, but that did not ease my fear or my frustration. I wanted the Counselor to guide me—to tell me everything was going to be all right again. Every time the Counselor spoke to me it strengthened my confidence. I had become very dependent on Him. I relied on Him to get me through the battle. I knew I had to quit acting like a baby and get myself together for the sake of the people of Soam and the Misfits. That's why I spent the afternoon meditating in a quiet area near the river.

It was getting dark. The others had built several fires around the camp. There were a few cooks in the brigade that Drakkar sent to me. You could smell food everywhere. I got in line for a plate, and everyone stepped aside to let me in front of them. I thought: *Huh— I could get used to this!* Being in charge did have its perks.

"Get plenty of meat. You need your protein," said the head cook.

I've never been much of a meat eater, but I knew the cook was right. I had to build up my energy for the next day. I ate as much as I could. I ate a lot of fruit—especially pomegranates—because I needed all the Vitamin C and antioxidants I could get.

"Tiffany, where are you?"

"Over here!" I could not see Vandy, but I knew what direction he was coming from by the sound of his voice. I met him halfway.

"Are you ready for tomorrow?" he asked.

"I'm not sure. I guess I'm as ready as I will ever be."

Harlow joined us. "You will do well, Tiffany. We knew from the start that you were the one."

"Thanks, guys." Their confidence in me boosted my confidence in myself. "We have come a long way since we first met. I think the world of all of you."

"We think the world of you too, Tiffany," Britny fluttered. "We couldn't have come this far without your help."

One of Drakkar's soldiers marched over with a pile of clothes. "I'm sorry I'm just getting these uniforms to you, but some were very difficult to make," he said with a wink. "Make sure they fit. If they don't, get with me immediately."

I laughed because I knew he was talking about the animals' uniforms being the difficult ones to make. The uniforms were made from leather. There was a leather helmet that covered the face, and a thick leather coat. The outfits fit everyone, including Vandy.

"It's not every day that a tailor can make an outfit that fits a meerkat perfectly," Vandy joked.

Ronin and Velvet also had outfits. It was not my intention for them to get into battle with me, but it's best to be prepared.

"You guys are staying here at camp and I mean it," I said sternly.

"Why can't we go? We have our uniforms, and we know the plan," said Velvet.

"Because you are my cats, and I don't want anything to happen to you."

"We don't want anything to happen to you either, but we should be together. Besides, I'm the one who came up with the battle strategy," said Ronin.

He did have a point. If something happened to me, they might not get back home, and they would be a big help distracting the Snardlins by having them chase them. "Okay, but you guys stay out of the fighting. You can scout the area and let us know of any impending dangers. And have the Snardlins chase you around like we discussed."

"Oh yeah, oh yeah, we fight tomorrow. Oh yeah, oh yeah, we fight tomorrow," sang Velvet with a little dance.

"You are going to do what tomorrow?" I asked.

"Oh yeah, oh yeah, we scout tomorrow," said Velvet in a more demure and less dance-y dance.

"That's what I thought you meant."

We all settled in for the night. As things quietened down, soldiers positioned themselves around the camp in case the Snardlins ambushed us. Velvet, Ronin, and I shared a tent with the Misfits.

I did not think I would sleep, but I was wrong. I fell into a deep sleep, probably because of so much stress about the looming battle.

I dreamed of my mother. She kept telling me over and over that I would win. She would often say the same thing before a gym meet. It was her way of helping me get over my lack of confidence. And it usually worked.

The next day, we woke early. The first thing I noticed when walking out of my tent was the ominous red sky. I remembered what the Counselor said: "Red skies in the morning indicate bad weather in the evening, which will be to your advantage."

Finally, the day of battle had arrived. There was no turning back. I felt strong and confident. I knew then that I was put there for a reason. I was chosen to help liberate Soam.

"Tiffany, come here," Vandy ordered.

"What is going on?" I asked.

"The Snardlins are starting to move out of the city walls and Drakkar doesn't want them to do that," Vandy spoke fast, either out of urgency or nervousness. "He wants to push them back, so we can sneak in unsuspectingly. Drakkar said that he will wave a torch when he is ready for us to go in."

"I guess we wait, then?"

"Yes."

"We should move up to the front of the camp since we will be going in first," Alanis suggested.

"Agreed," said Harlow.

We grabbed our gear and walked to the front of the camp, settling on a ridge overlooking Snard. I could see the Snardlins lined up in front of their city and on top of the city walls waiting for Drakkar to attack. There were so many, I could not count them all. The city looked like an impenetrable fortress.

Drakkar's army was also menacing. The horses, with their riders, were all ranked in a perfect line across the desert dunes. Then I looked to the front and saw Drakkar standing in his chariot, ready to conquer.

"I think I should fly into Snard to get an idea how the Snardlins will be positioned on the inside," said Britny.

"I think she's right," Alanis said. "If we get into trouble, Britny might be able to help us find a way out."

"Okay," I agreed. "Go, and be careful. See if there are any passageways or tunnels that we can use to avoid being seen once we get into the city."

Britny flew off to Snard as we waited and watched for Drakkar to attack.

Then we heard battle horns. Britny returned and said, "They're going in now."

I looked to the sky and saw thousands of arrows coming from Drakkar's men. It looked as if the sky was overtaken by a swarm of bees. The arrows went high then rained down on the city. You could see the Snardlins fall by the hundreds. After several waves of arrows, Drakkar and his army swarmed in. They bolted across the desert on horseback and chariots. I couldn't see much because of the dust the mighty horses had stirred up.

The Snardlins stood on top of the city walls shooting arrows and throwing spears. When the dust settled, I saw Drakkar and his soldiers fighting off the Snardlins with their swords. The Snardlins were much bigger than the Drakkar soldiers, so I could distinguish between them easily. They fought for hours. Eventually, the Snardlins were pushed back into their city, and that's where they encamped.

Drakkar's army pulled back from the city walls. It was beginning to get dark, and I could feel the weather changing. The wind picked up. I could see lightning far off in the distance. The skies grew dark and ominous. My heart raced. I started to sweat. I could feel the adrenaline kick in, just like it would before a gymnastics competition. But this time I was more fearful.

"Make sure you have your suits on and are completely covered," said one of the soldiers.

"Why?" I asked.

"The Snardlins have a keen sense of smell. Because of poor eyesight, they rely on their smell more than they do on their eyes."

I immediately thought of what The Counselor had said about the storm being to our advantage. The rain will hinder the Snardlins' sight, but more importantly, it will mitigate their sense of smell. That would be to our benefit.

The storm drew closer. The lightning calmed, but the rain grew heavier. "Gather your weapons. Get your horses ready," Vandy ordered.

I got my gear together, grabbed my knife and my slingshot, and secured my gumdrops in my pouch. As I did, I noticed something strange. The gumdrops were glowing, but clear. I had never seen them without some color.

They blinked in sequence, then stopped. I was not sure if that was a good sign or a bad sign. I picked up my slingshot and saw something else. It, too, was clear and blinking. The slingshot twinkled like the gumdrops and suddenly stopped. The slingshot and the gumdrops were in sync with each other. I pulled the sling back and it sparkled. It also shot a beam of bright light in the direction of my aim. I knew at that very moment that I had everything I needed to defend our army.

"Drakkar has the torch in his hand. It looks like we are going in soon," said Boris.

"Get ready!" I said.

I thought to myself, *is that all you've got? That's your speech? 'Get ready?'* I looked at everyone and cleared my throat.

"Wait, wait everyone! We are now here. Some of us never could have imagined that we would be involved in a mighty battle. A battle that has nothing to do with some of us, in the sense that we are from different times or different worlds. Soam wasn't even in my vocabulary until lately. The Soamites were exiled out of their own land because the Snardlins wanted them under their rule.

"This could happen to any of us. We could all be exiled from our homelands. We fight today for freedom. We fight for compassion. We fight for the basic reason of truth.

"What is truth, you ask? Truth is the foundation of what is right. Some cannot see the truth because they are blind. The Snardlins cannot see well in the literal since because of their poor eyesight. They cannot see truth because they love the darkness. We are up against the very axis of evil. If we have truth, believe in justice, and believe in what is good—we will not fail!"

Everyone cheered. I looked deep into Strider's eyes and the rest of the Hakkamadoos. I saw no fear. Drakkar's soldiers fixated on Snard. The Misfits looked the most confident than I had ever seen them.

We were ready. The time had come. I could feel the presence of the Counselor around me. For the first time in my life, I was fearless. As everyone stood in silence, I prayed, "Counselor, be with us and protect us. We ask for your guidance and wisdom. We trust in you and have faith in you. We cannot do this alone. Show us the way to victory, show the Snardlins the truth."

14 TAKING SNARD

We were about to start our march toward Snard, but I remembered I had left my leather helmet in the tent. I went back to get it and found it beside my blanket. When I exited the tent, a cold breeze hit me in the face. A huge black scorpion scurried in front of me, and I paused. It raised itself up on its tail and grew taller until it morphed into a human.

It was Orianthia.

"Hello, Tiffany," she shrieked. "Where are you off to?"

Stunned, I couldn't speak. That lasted only a second. I snapped out of my stupor and said, "I'm off to defeat the Snardlins."

"Why would you do that?"

"They are evil. They've forced the citizens of Soam out of their own country."

"If the Soamites would have obeyed the king, they'd still be in their own country."

"The Soamites had their own king, King Zirdak. The Snardlins took everything from the Soamites, and I intend to take it back." I looked deep into the queen's eyes and saw her pupils dilate to an ominous black. Her eyes shifted back and forth as she spoke.

"Tiffany, I can give you anything you want. I can give you any kingdom to rule. I can give you the world."

"Desiring everything in this world is what causes evil. Being good is rewarding. Being evil and enjoying it is a façade."

"You are young, dear," the queen smiled gallantly. "I can make you wealthy. Everyone will bow at your feet. Everyone will want to be you. You will have the worlds at your fingertips. You will be the most powerful girl in the universe, all you need to do is submit to me. It will change your life."

Orianthia's eyes flew open wide. I gazed into her dazzling green eyes and felt my body weaken. Something about her stare mesmerized me. I considered her offer and, for a moment, wondered if I should take it.

I sensed that she spoke into my mind without mouthing words. I thought that maybe she could get me out of the mess I was in, and I could go home. Images of my parents flashed in my mind. They said, "Listen to her, Tiffany. We want you back home."

Her power was so strong it was nearly irresistible. Her temptations were beginning to win me over. Then another force broke the spell. A power welled up from inside me that melted the image of my parents like candle wax. That stronger power pulled me away from Orianthia and I felt temptation disappear. My focus became clearer.

When the queen's power left my mind, something odd appeared. A kaleidoscope of butterflies swarmed around me. There must have been thousands. They swarmed around my body as if protecting me. The colors were amazing. Vibrant blue, yellow, and orange swirls beamed all around me. I could not see Orianthia through all the butterflies.

I felt so comfortable and guarded. Then I heard Gem's voice.

"Tiffany, do not listen to the queen. She wants to destroy you. She sees the good in you and hates it. She will try anything to bring you into her world and tear you apart."

"Get away from her," screamed Orianthia, her voice taking on a deeper, more ominous tone. As she spoke, her eyes grew darker, and I could barely see them through the butterflies. "Come now, Tiffany. You must come with me."

The butterflies built a wall between Orianthia and me. I ran back to the troops Drakkar had given me to command. A loud clap of thunder exploded near my ear and a black streak shot through the sky. I fell into position in front of the soldiers under my command. Drakkar waved the torch back and forth to signal our time to move. I gave the order, and we rode into darkness.

I'm sure everyone thought the same thing: would we make it out alive? But those thoughts dissipated quickly as we reached the river. With thunder in the distance, the wind blew harder, and it began to rain.

We waded through the warm water, about chest high on me, and crept in slowly so as not to make any noise. Torches kept the city lit. I could hear voices echoing off the city walls as we entered through the tunnel. Water dripped from the tunnel's ceiling, which was musty and smelled like mildew. Velvet and Ronin rode on one of the Hakkamadoos' back. We came to a walkway on one side of the tunnel.

"Get off here," I ordered. "Try to find any passageways that could lead us out of trouble. I love you guys." Velvet and Ronin leaped off the Hakkamadoos' back and ran out of sight.

Britny landed on my shoulder and said, "Tiffany, there is a staircase about a hundred yards and to the left that leads up to the main part of the city gate. There are no Snardlins guarding that area. It could be a good place to catch the Snardlins off guard."

"Okay, we will go in here," I said. "Send word to the other brigade to keep pushing through the tunnel until they are inside the city." Britny flew back to inform them of the plan.

I could hear voices from inside the city getting louder. I sent Harlow and Alanis to search out the compound. We ascended the staircase and saw shadows of bodies moving. In the distance, I heard boots stomping the brick-lined city streets. I saw a silhouette of Drakkar going in at the front of the city. The shadows moved away from where we were standing.

Drakkar pulled the Snardlins farther away from us. I knew it was time to go in. I ordered the troops I commanded to storm the city. I pulled out my slingshot, and everyone followed me in. We came in fast and caught the Snardlins off guard. The Snardlins had gone to fight Drakkar at the front of the city.

The fight was on. I ordered the Hakkamadoos to follow me to the west part of the city. I ordered Vandy to lead Drakkar's soldiers to the south side of the city because more Snardlins were there.

A Snardlin came straight for me with a sword and swung at my head. To keep from being sliced in two, I performed a couple of backward handsprings. He came at me again. I didn't want to use the gumdrops unless I had to and did my best to not draw attention to them. I knew if the Snardlins saw the gumdrops, they would all come after me.

I grabbed a pebble from my pouch and loaded my slingshot, then pulled it back to fire. It sparkled. I shot the Snardlin right between the eyes. He fell to the ground. I ran past his body to a moat between our division and what looked like the entrance to a palace. I surmised it must have been the king's residence because I could see it was opulent and distinctly more lavish than the other buildings around it. The building was lined in ornate gold filigree. There were beautiful fountains spewing water in pools that surrounded the compound. There were watchtowers above that had flags with giant red S letters on them.

It was dark. The rain was heavy. I saw what looked like huge boulders laid out like a bridge across the moat. I thought, *I will cross the moat over those boulders.* I jumped on the first one; it did not seem hard like a rock's surface should be. I jumped on the second one and it moved beneath my feet. Then I found myself lifted into the air and landing in the water. I went under and bobbed back to the surface.

"Yum, yum!" The sound came from one of the boulders. I had not seen nor heard of a Yum Yum since the first day I met the Misfits. I did remember how fierce they were.

One Yum Yum came after me. I swam as fast as I could to get away from it. I reached some rocks at the edge of the moat, but the Yum Yum caught up with me. I reached for my slingshot but discovered it was caught on a rock.

The Yum Yum came straight for my head with its mouth wide open. Just before it reached my head, a voice said, "Extraordinary!" Then I heard the Yum Yum squeal. Cece was tearing the eye out of the Yum Yum with his claws. Blinded by the loss of its eyes, the Yum Yum swam off, shrieking and squealing thunderously.

Cece landed on my shoulder. "What are you doing here, Cece?" I asked.

"Cece wants to help. Cece sorry for what he did. Cece did not know what he was doing. Luna Toosa made Cece mean."

I grabbed him and hugged him. I must have embarrassed him because his feathers turned red.

"Follow me," said Cece.

I climbed the rocks back to level ground and ran as fast as I could to catch up with him. When I did catch up with him, I saw that he had taken a torch that had been lighting one of the passageways off the wall. He hit a Snardlin in the head with the torch. The Snardlin's hair caught fire.

Cece repeated that maneuver multiple times. The Snardlins ran frantically through the city streets, screaming and burning. A couple ran past me and jumped into the moat. And the Yum Yums welcomed them. Cece's combat skills were impressive.

I heard someone behind me say, "Watch out, Tiffany!"

Then I heard a whizzing sound behind me. Immediately, I hit the ground just as a thud pounded my ears. I looked up and saw an arrow stuck in the wall. Turning around, I saw a Snardlin headed toward me. At that moment, a silhouette appeared behind the wall. The silhouette grew bigger as it moved toward the Snardlin. Someone yelled as the silhouetted figure slammed the Snardlin in the head with a sword. The Snardlin's head went flying.

The figure turned around and asked, "Are you all right, Tiffany?"

"Allasso!" I ran and grabbed his arm. "I thought you were dead! What happened?"

"I will tell you later. We have work to do!"

"This way, guys!" yelled Vandy.

Vandy and a company of Hakkamadoos were on the other side of the city street. Drakkar's soldiers fought a battalion of Snardlins near the main city gate. Allasso and I ran toward Vandy. Then I saw Cece lying lifeless against a wall, his feathers solid white. I ran to him and cried out, "Cece, are you alright? Can you hear me?" His little body lay still. As I held back my tears, I picked him up and put him in my pouch. I ran to catch up with the rest of the unit as the battle intensified. It was finally time for some gumdrops.

I pulled one out and the weirdest thing happened. I heard Carly Simon's song "You're So Vain" playing in my head. That was my grandmother's favorite song. You would think that in the heat of battle the last song that would come to mind is "You're So Vain," but that's what happened.

Snardlins were everywhere. I shot a gumdrop and hit one, taking out five others with the explosion. I saw Vandy walking through the smoke. The explosion had singed his hair and left his helmet smoking. I couldn't help but laugh.

"Watch out, Tiffany! Those gumdrops are dangerous!" Vandy shouted.

Velvet came running out of the smoke. "This way, Tiffany."

I ran after her. We went through a passageway and up several flights of stairs. When we got to the top step, Velvet stopped. "The King is in there, Tiffany," she whispered.

Sure enough. There he was. The wicked King Arista himself.

I grabbed a gumdrop and loaded it. When I pulled the strap on the slingshot, it lit up brighter than ever. As I took aim, something hit my legs, knocking me to the ground. The gumdrop went flying. It rolled into the king's quarters, and King Arista picked it up.

"Luna Toosa," the king said, in a trance. He took off with the gumdrop. I jumped up after realizing that a piece of debris had knocked me to the ground. I quickly loaded my slingshot and fired at the king as he ran away. The gumdrop took part of a wall down in the king's quarters. As the dust settled, I could see the king had escaped.

Ronin came running up the stairs, followed by Strider and some of the Hakkamadoos. "We must attack from the top of the city walls," yelled Strider. We ran to the edge of the walls and fired at the Snardlins, taking out many of them. I looked to the center of town and noticed that the citizens of Snard were dancing and partying in the streets. They acted as if they didn't know there was a battle going on. The city was so big, so vast, the Snardlins couldn't hear or see the fierce fighting.

The battle intensified. I could see Drakkar and his soldiers moving in. Allasso wiped out Snardlins left and right. I fired gumdrops at the Snardlins and watched them explode. The rain fell harder. And you could tell the Snardlins were having a difficult time seeing.

"Look, Tiffany," said Harlow.

I looked at the wall in the eastern part of the city. Orianthia stood on the city wall. She made eye contact with me and looked angry. I shot a gumdrop at her. As the gumdrop drew closer to her, its pace slowed. She caught it in her hand, glared at me, and smiled. Then disappeared.

I knew then that I had a problem. Two of the gumdrops were in the hands of evil.

"Duck everyone!" Alanis screamed as she ran across the city wall behind us. I looked to the sky and hundreds of flaming arrows were raining down from Drakkar's army. We all ran and dove under a ledge on the giant wall. I could hear the arrows hitting the Snardlins, one by one. Once they stopped falling, we ran back out to fight.

I saw several Snardlins looking at the sky. Shadows drew closer. The rain fell heavier and harder. I could not make out what was going on, the rain was so thick. But I could see Snardlins being snatched up, lifted off the ground, and disappearing into the night sky. It was Abby and the albatrosses, carrying them off with their claws.

Abby flew in and landed. "Tiffany, come with me."

I leaped onto Abby's back, and we ascended into the night sky. Vandy and some of the others did the same. We climbed high enough for the Snardlin arrows to miss us. Then Abby nosedived, heading straight for the city. I loaded my slingshot and fired at a pack of Snardlins running for their lives. A huge explosion leveled dozens of them upon impact.

Abby sped through the city, picking up and throwing Snardlins one by one. Drakkar's army had contained the entrance to the city and created havoc in the streets. Drakkar himself fought King Arista in the courtyard. They both used swords, but Drakkar seemed to have the edge.

By that time, the whole city was in chaos. The Snardlins fled from the city. But many of them were still fighting. They were not going to give up easily.

"Help!" Velvet screamed.

I saw a Snardlin had her in his paw. "Bring me down, Abby!"

Abby dropped me to the ground. I ran as fast as I could and jumped off a wall onto the Snardlin's neck. He let Velvet go, but he slammed me to the ground. I lay there in a pool of water, almost out of breath. The rain poured down on my body, and I couldn't move. Everything was a blur. That was the last thing I remembered.

When I woke up, I was being dragged through the city streets by the hair of my head. I could feel the stone-lined street ripping through my armor. Blood poured down my face. I could barely see in front of me. But my vision improved enough that I saw that it was a Snardlin pulling me toward a building. He dragged me up a flight of stairs, banging my body against the brick steps. I reached for a gumdrop, but I knew if I shot him at that close range, it would kill us both. I pulled the gumdrop out and whistled. The Snardlin turned around and immediately let go of me.

"Luna Toosa," he said, gazing at the gumdrop and taking it from my hand. He fell into a trance.

I stood and ran. Once at a safe distance, I pulled out a gumdrop and aimed for the one the Snardlin held in his hand. I fired and hit the gumdrop. Both gumdrops exploded and the Snardlin went with them. The shockwave was so intense it blew me off the ground, and I went flying. Landing in the street, I slid for several feet on my side. My leather jacket was ripped to shreds and I bled all over my body from the injuries.

As I lay in the street, unable to move, the rain pouring over me, I saw the fiery arrows flying overhead and heard screaming all around. I could feel my strength leaving my body. *Is this it?* I thought. *Am I done?*

I thought about my family. I could see Mom's face and started to cry. I felt that I would never see her again. I had remembered my last gymnastics meet. It wasn't a good day. My mom said, "Tiffany, get up and fight for what you want! You are stronger than you think, my little warrior."

It was the last thing I heard before slipping out of consciousness.

15 NEVER DEFEATED

"Tiffany, wake up."

I heard the voice, but it seemed far off. I felt as if I was going away. I felt as if I was leaving my body, moving through something I couldn't understand. Without fear. It seemed as if I belonged to where I was going. I hadn't felt like that since the butterflies.

Then I heard the voice again. "Tiffany, wake up. It is not your time. You have many things to do."

I woke up and saw Gem, the butterfly, glowing brightly. I was also glowing. Then the glow slowly left us, leaving me feeling energized. My strength returned.

"Thank you, Gem," I said, after coming to my senses.

"You do not have to thank me, Tiffany. That is why I'm here, to look after you and to watch over you."

Britny landed on my shoulder. In a panic, she spoke faster than usual. "Tiffany, the Snardlins have trapped Vandy and the Hakkamadoos in the tunnel south of the gate. They cannot hold the Snardlins off much longer and have no place to go."

I looked around to see where Gem was, but she had gone.

"Okay, let's go." Britny took off from my shoulder. I leapt up and ran after Britny, catching up with her after running a couple of hundred yards. I managed to make it to the south end of the city in record time. Sure enough,

Vandy and the Hakkamadoos were trapped. I couldn't see Drakkar or his army, so I figured they had their hands full with the Snardlins.

I saw some ropes that looked like they were being used for construction hanging from the city wall. I grabbed one of the ropes and tugged on it to see if it was secure. Confident that it was, I stretched and took hold of the rope as high up as my arms would reach, planting my feet against the wall and scaling the wall. It was difficult and scary when I looked down to see how high I had climbed.

I was three quarters up the wall when a Snardlin peaked his head over the top. He grabbed the rope and pulled me up the wall faster. My feet could barely keep up, he was pulling me so fast.

I twisted the rope around my wrist so I wouldn't fall and dropped my feet so they would dangle. The front of my body sliding parallel to the wall. Using my free hand, I was able to grab a gumdrop out of my pouch and put it in my mouth. Then, using the same hand, I took hold of my slingshot. As the Snardlin pulled me up the wall, I held the slingshot with my hand holding the rope and loaded the gumdrop in my mouth. I pulled the sling with my free hand and took aim at the Snardlin on the top of the wall.

I fired.

The gumdrop missed the Snardlin directly but hit the top of the wall and exploded bricks everywhere. Some of the bricks hit the Snardlin in the face. It fell off the wall toward me. I kicked off the wall to allow the Snardlin to pass and it landed in the street with a splatter.

Taking a deep breath, I put away my slingshot and began to pull myself up the wall again. When I reached the top of the wall, I stretched my arm over the ledge and pulled my body over the wall. Some scaffolding_nearby gave me an idea.

Alanis, Velvet, Ronin, and Harlow came running on the street below.

"The Snardlins are losing to Drakkar's army," Alanis shouted. "They are fighting in the heart of the city, and many of the Snardlins are running out of town."

"Okay, you guys stay out of harm's way," I said. "I will catch up with you later."

Britny asked, "What are we going to do, Tiffany?"

"I have an idea," I said.

I ran toward the scaffolding. Several huge boulders lay on the top of it. Huge ropes held the scaffolding together. If I could reach the ropes and cut them, I knew the boulders would fall and crush the Snardlins below. But could I do it before the Snardlins closed in on Vandy and the Hakkamadoos? If I failed, the Snardlins would surely crush Vandy's element.

I ran along the top of the wall as fast as I could. When I reached the edge, I somersaulted and landed on the scaffolding adjacent to the scaffolding the boulders were on. The scaffolding was about fifty feet above ground. One of the Snardlins heard me. He pointed. That instant, arrows began flying toward me, whizzing by me from every angle.

I grabbed my knife and cut one of the ropes as an arrow pierced my leg. It didn't go through, but it did lock in on a muscle. I screamed. I once tore my hamstring during a gymnastics competition, but the arrow in my leg made that feel like a pinprick. It felt like someone took an ice pick and jabbed it into my leg, then raked it through the muscle. That caused the Snardlins to become even more aggressive.

Wrapping my fingers around the arrow, I yanked it out of my leg. The pain was so intense it felt like someone had pulled the muscle out of my leg. I tore a piece of my shirt off, made a tourniquet, and wrapped it around my leg. I low-crawled across the scalfolding so I wouldn't be an easy target. The arrows continued to fly at me, hitting the scaffolding. It sounded like a woodpecker on a hollow tree. One of the arrows made it through a crack between two boards on the bottom end of the scaffolding. Getting caught in the boards, it pricked the tip of my nose. Ignoring the bleeding, I pressed on until I made it to the ropes. I put my knife to one of them and cut it.

A small boulder came flying overhead from one of Drakkar's catapults and hit the scaffolding. It rocked back and forth. I slid off the side, grabbing the edge with one hand and hanging on for dear life. With my knife still in my hand, I jammed it into the side of the wood scaffolding so I wouldn't lose it and grabbed part of the rope rigging connecting the scaffolding to the wall of the building. I then pulled myself upright on the scaffolding, thankful I didn't fall.

Slowly, I maneuvered myself back to the boulders and cut the second rope with my knife. The boulders fell wiping out several more Snardlins. That was the break Vandy and the Hakkamadoos needed.

Strider mowed through the Snardlins below one by one. The Snardlins retreated to the front of the city as Vandy and the Hakkamadoos chased after them. I turned and saw Orianthia standing in a dark alleyway aligned with block walls. Between us were a pile of dead Snardlins in the streets. Rubble lay everywhere. Ashes from the city's burning fires fell into the path that lay between us. In her hand was the gumdrop she had stolen from me. She taunted me with it.

Slowly, I worked my way over to her. I climbed through the rubble dodging the fires and debris that littered the streets, straddling Snardlin bodies as I pushed my way through. While stepping over a dead Snardlin, I felt something grab my ankle. A Snardlin lying on its back covered in blood jerked my ankle and I fell on my backside. The Snardlin tugged on me, trying to pull me toward it. I reached for my knife but dropped it, and it fell from my reach.

I tried to fight against the Snardlin's tugs, but it was too strong. My hands were scraping the bricks on the street as I slid closer to his hungry mouth. The Snardlin grabbed my other leg. Though he was covered in blood and struggling to breathe, he began to laugh. At that moment, I looked to my left and saw a brick lying beside a dead Snardlin. I grabbed the brick, jumped to my feet, and hit the Snardlin in the head. He stopped laughing and let me go of his hold. Finally, I made it through the maze of destruction and stood face to face with Orianthia.

She stood gallant and sturdy with a sinister smile on her face. Her eyes turned to fire and her voice sounded like a demon's. "I gave you many opportunities to come my way, Tiffany, and you've resisted. This is your last chance. Let me give you your own kingdom."

Something breathed hard down my neck. Whatever it was gave off an awful smell. I turned and saw King Arista. His eyes captivated me with fire, and he was bigger than the average Snardlin.

"Tiffany, come with me. Let's rule the world together," the queen chanted. "We all have a gumdrop now, and we only need three to complete the Luna Toosa."

"What is the Luna Toosa?" I asked.

"Luna Toosa is the most powerful force there is." Orianthia chose her words carefully. "We could rule the world, defeat any kingdom. But there must be a mortal human willing to be a part of the change."

"That's why you keep bothering me. You want me to help you in your sinister plot to turn the world into darkness. No, I don't think so."

"Okay, then. We will take your gumdrops and find another mortal soul to help us."

I gulped. For a moment, I thought I would wet my pants. King Arista reached for my pouch. I hit the ground in a full split. He missed and I rolled between his legs. As I rolled, I grabbed a stone from the ground and shot it from my slingshot, hitting King Arista in the back. He fell to the the ground. I ran in the opposite direction and thought I'd escaped, but the queen cut me off. It was as if she had appeared out of nowhere.

"You can't run from me, Tiffany!"

I thought, *this is one persistent and wicked queen.*

"Flee from her!" Allasso shouted from a street that led to the alleyway. He charged Orianthia, but she extended her hand and Allasso went sliding across the ground.

He stood again and ran faster, but the queen stomped her foot. The bricks lining the city streets rose and shot toward Allasso. All the bricks knocked him to the ground. Then they gathered around him and buried him.

I didn't know what to do. I was over my head. I then remembered the riddle and whispered to myself, "As bark grows on a tree, wherever your mind may be, if your mind starts to stray, let the gumdrops show the way."

As if with minds of their own, the gumdrops came out of my pouch and circled me as the bricks had circled Allasso. They blinked a neon blue. They moved faster, like race cars on a speedway, circling around me. Forming themselves from the ground to the top of my head, they circled me like a wagon train. Before I knew it, a neon blue blanket of light surrounded my body.

I rose off the ground. Orianthia screamed. She began to spin, looking like a figure skater. Faster and faster she spun until she became a funnel, a tornado of fire, and shot upward through the night sky.

I rose over the city. Arrows on the ground pointed the way that I should go, as if leading me to safety. They were like holograms amid a sea of neon blue gumdrops. I descended toward the ground and the gumdrops quit glowing. When the color dissipated, they flew back into my pouch. I walked to where the arrows had been pointing. When I turned the corner, I saw Drakkar and his army fighting what few Snardlins were left.

Standing in the city street reflecting on what had just happened, voices droning on in the background, I tried to make out what they were saying. They grew louder. I finally recognized them as the residents of Snard chanting, "Goonatay! Goonatay! Goonatay!"

A crowd of people formed at the west end of the city. They stood beside a huge gate with fifty or more Snardlins.

The chants grew louder. "Goonatay! Goonatay! Goonatay!"

Then I heard a thump! And another thump!

A creature let out an ear-piercing scream, like the sound of Godzilla in those old movies.

The gate lifted. Two huge glowing eyes made their way to the entrance. Thump! Thump! Thump! I heard another scream. A creature's head peered through the open gate.

The creature walked into the street. It was a giant Red Gargoyle Gecko. I had studied Gargoyle Geckos in science class a couple of years ago in school. What made this creature different than the small ones I studied was its wings, and its enormous size. It stood at least twenty feet and was more than fifty feet long.

The crowd fell silent. Kneeling on the ground, they chanted in low voices "Goonatay! Goonatay! Goonatay!"

The creature screamed again. It flapped its wings and lifted itself off the ground. Its tail swung around and swiped a bunch of the Snardlins along with some of the citizens, slamming them against the city walls. It was obvious this creature called Goonatay didn't discriminate against its victims.

I watched the Goonatay fly toward me and land directly in front of me. When it landed, the ground shook like an earthquake. I froze in fear. The bright red creature with gray eyes lit up from the inside out as if on fire. Its scales, slick and shiny like pewter, seemed to hold the fire like a torch, giving rise to its flames in a most peculiar way.

Its head lowered until its eyes met mine, and it sniffed at me like a dog sniff's a rosebush. I couldn't move, so scared to death I was. The creature glared at me strangely as if as amazed by me as I was by it.

My body shook all over. The creature walked around me a couple of times before speaking. "Uoy era eht eno ot reuqnoc lla sdlrow, Tiffany Triumph."

"How do you know my name?" I asked.

The creature looked at me without a word and walked away. It walked toward the Misfits and Drakkar's army. Thump! Thump! Thump! As it walked, it released another ear-piercing scream.

"Fire!" I recognized Drakkar's voice.

"No!" I screamed.

Before I could stop them, Drakkar's army attacked the creature. Arrows went flying. Drakkar's men also went flying as the creature swiped them with its tail. I ran to where I could get Drakkar's attention, but it was too late. The fight was on.

The creature wailed in pain as arrows pierced its body. It swiped its tail, crashing one of the city walls and turning it into a pile of rubble. I saw Velvet, Ronin, and the Misfits hiding in an alley on an adjacent street and ran to them.

"Drakkar must stop fighting the creature!" I yelled.

"What? Stop attacking! What do you mean, Tiffany?" asked Vandy, "This creature is trying to kill us all!"

"I think the creature is good. It knows my name. It was trying to tell me something."

"Why is it attacking Drakkar?" asked Britny.

"Drakkar and his army attacked the creature first," said Harlow.

The fifty Snardlins that returned to the city took the opportunity to charge Drakkar and his army while occupied with the Goonatay. Velvet, Ronin, and Alanis took off out of the alley. As if they remembered the battle plan, all three cats ran in and out of the Snardlin pack gaining the Snardlins' attention.

Several Snardlins broke from the pack and chased the cats. Harlow darted out of the alley and a couple of Snardlins took off after her. Several Snardlins swatted their arms in the air as Britny zoomed around their heads.

Strider and the Hakkamadoos jumped from one of the city walls, mowing down the Snardlins with their swords in the process. Several of the Hakkamadoos used Charan moves while wrestling the Snardlins to the ground, knocking them off their feet. Boris ran around stabbing Snardlins' feet with his little sword.

"Come on, Vandy. Follow me," I said, running out of the alley. I headed straight to a Snardlin standing in the street about to throw an axe at Drakkar. I grabbed a gumdrop out of my pouch and shot the Snardlin as it lifted its arms in the air to fling the axe. The gumdrop hit the Snardlin and blew it to pieces. The axe flew high into the air and landed on another Snardlin's head, splitting it wide open.

Vandy grabbed that Snardlin's knife and threw it at another Snardlin, slitting its throat. The Snardlin fell to the ground gasping for air as Vandy darted off to another one chasing Harlow.

Drakkar and his men were no match for the Goonatay. The creature forced them out of the city gate. The Goonatay's tail destroyed every city wall it swiped. Rubble and dust clouded the air all around. The Snardlins were confused because of their poor eyesight. Several of them wandered too close to the Goonatay and were swiped by its tail. It sent them flying through the city, slamming them against one of the huge walls supporting the gate. Drakkar and his men managed to get through the gate before it, too, collapsed.

The creature flapped its wings, slowly lifting it into the sky. It flew higher as it flapped its wings. Its body now was entirely consumed by fire, but the fire wasn't destroying the creature. It was as if the Goonatay controlled the fire.

It flew in circles around the city skyline. Arrows flew from Drakkar's soldiers, but the creature was too high in the sky. It hovered in one spot above me, looked at me, and shouted, "Ew lliw teem niaga, Tiffany Triumph!" Then it screamed and flew out of sight.

Drakkar and his men returned to the city and fought the remaining Snardlins, who were losing. A few of them vacated the city. I looked at the gate and it was empty. All the citizens were gone.

The fighting came to a halt. Strider and the Hakkamadoos approached me. Britny flew up and asked, "Where's Ronin, Velvet, and Alanis?"

"Here we are!" Alanis shouted. Harlow was right behind them with Vandy.

"Hey guys! Are there any Snardlins left on the south side of the city?" Boris asked.

"I don't think so," said Strider. "I saw the last one fall to the ground."

Drakkar raised his sword above his head and slammed it through a statue of King Arista. As he did, he shouted, "No more!" Then he walked toward the city gate. When he reached it, he turned and raised his hand, giving me a thumbs up. I signaled an acceptance he turned and walked out of the gate.

"Where is King Arista?" I asked.

"I saw him sneaking out of the city through a passageway," said Britny.

I knew the gumdrops would never be seen again unless they could be used for evil purposes. I felt like we had won the battle, but I also felt like it was accompanied by a great loss. Two gumdrops were gone, but three could change the world in a bad way.

"Where is Allasso?" asked Vandy. "I saw him fighting with us."

"That's right," I said. "Follow me."

We ran to where I had last seen Allasso. We started pulling rocks off a mound of rubble in the street. When we caught sight of Allasso, he pulled himself out of the pile and thanked us.

"Are you all right, Allasso? Strider asked.

"Yes, I'm all right. My head hurts and I'm a little dizzy, but I will be fine."

"What happened to you?" Vandy asked him. "The last time we saw you, a Sand Livid had pulled you under the sand."

"Yes, the Sand Livid did take me under and swallowed me whole. Once I was in its stomach, I cut my way out with a knife. Those things are tough. I must have spent a couple of days digging myself out."

"We are glad you are alive, Allasso," I said. "We can't thank you enough for your help."

"I will always help those who want to do good. I'm glad that Snard has been defeated. It is bittersweet. This was my home. My culture. But politics, greed, and power destroyed it."

"Where will you go now?" asked Britny.

"I had planned on leaving Snard for a long time," Allasso told us. "I made a home for my family in the countryside. That is where I plan to settle down. My work here is done. I must go now. Good luck to you all."

We said our goodbyes and Allasso left Snard. Strider and the Hakkamadoos headed back to camp.

"You did it, Tiffany," Vandy said, congratulating me. "I knew you were special."

"We did it, Vandy." I smiled. "We all did it together."

Britny landed on my shoulder and was about to say something when I heard another voice say, "Extraordinary!" Cece popped his head out of my pouch.

"I thought you were dead, Cece," I laughed. "You lay lifeless in the street and couldn't move."

"Cece okay. Head sore, though." He rubbed a big knot on his head, and we all laughed.

"I must get back to camp," Vandy said. "Drakkar is going to sign the decree to let the Soamites return to their home and live as they please."

"That's great! " I said.

"This has been a long journey, Tiffany," Britny chimed in, "but we made it."

"Yes, we did." I said with a giggle.

Britny flew with Cece back to camp. I sat on the city wall and pondered my future. Then I heard a voice say, "You did it, kid!"

I turned and there was Englow. I ran and gave him a big hug, with tears flowing down my face. "I could not have done it without you, Englow. I'm so glad you're here. What a battle! Did you see the Goonatay?"

"Yes, yes, Goonatay," Englow said pulling out his eyepiece and wiping it with a cloth. "It's very sad, the story about the Goonatay."

"What do you mean, Englow?"

"Well, Goonatay had a mate many, many years ago. Her mate was a creature just like her. He was captured by a wicked king named Honin the third. King Honin ruled over the Ishman Kingdom. It was one of the most powerful kingdoms the worlds have ever known."

Englow sat on a boulder and continued, "You see, Tiffany. Goonatay is attracted to greatness, and so was her mate. He was lured into the Ishman Kingdom because he could sense its power."

"What happened to Goonatay's mate?"

"He wandered into the town where he was held captive by a huge net and tranquilized. King Honin knew the legend of the Red Gargoyle. He wanted the power of the unquenchable fire the creature had."

"I saw that fire. It was like Goonatay was wrapped in a fireball," I said looking into the sky.

"Very powerful force it is. So powerful it destroyed an entire country," Englow said.

"An entire country?" I exclaimed.

"Yes! King Honin killed Goonatay's mate and tried to remove the unquenchable fire from him. When he did, the explosion could be felt in different worlds, not just this one."

"How did Goonatay know my name?' I asked.

Englow stood up. "Tiffany, Goonatay normally speaks in a language no one understands. The legend says whoever can figure out her language will have her as a guardian for life."

"Hmm… she did know my name."

"That's what I find interesting, Tiffany. She said your name where you could understand."

"I didn't understand the rest of what she said, though."

Englow winked and smiled. "Maybe you will," he said.

"But what now?" I asked.

"You have a lot more to do, Tiffany. There is much evil that must be destroyed."

"Perhaps I'm not the best person for that job. I let two of the gumdrops get in the hands of King Arista and The Black Mountain Queen."

"We do have a problem there," Englow admitted. "But I assure you, Tiffany, evil will eventually find its end. Always remember, the world you are in will change. Cultures change. Societies change."

"Do not conform your thoughts or principles to satisfy what is wrong. There will be a day when what seems right will be culturally wrong, and what is wrong will be generally accepted."

"But Englow, am I right to fight against what is wrong? I have helped destroy many Snardlins. Was killing them wrong?"

"There are times when drastic measures must be taken to defeat evil. No one should ever stop you or anyone else from protecting themselves. If it takes a weapon to win, so be it."

"When leadership tries to take your rights from you, that is when it is time to stand up and fight for your freedom." Englow continued, and I listened intently. "Authority should never control how we live or believe. We have laws we must obey, but that is where control stops.

"As you go through the worlds, one thing you will see. Societies will try to change the truth. But the truth cannot change. Truth was, truth is, and truth will always be. No matter what one's worldview might be, truth does not conform."

"Will I see you again, Englow? ... Englow?" He was gone.

As I sat alone looking over the once great city of Snard, I couldn't help but wonder, *where will I go next? What world exists beyond the next window of time? Will I find the correct window of time that will allow me to return to my family?*

I stood. As the sun rose and the rays touched my face, I looked beyond the devastated and desolate city and could see nothing but desert and the horizon. I could see the heat rising off the sand as the day began.

My mind settled, and my thoughts focused on the victory. Yes, we did liberate Soam, and the Soamites will be able to return to their homeland. I was proud of that. But I couldn't help but think what I had sacrificed. Ronin and Velvet stood beside me on the wall. I looked at them and they looked at me. Without saying a word, I could read their thoughts. When *will we return home?*

THE END

ABOUT THE AUTHOR

Rory has been a fan of fantasy novels since an early age. He loves writing and creating new worlds for readers to enjoy. When not writing, Rory enjoys being on his horse rescue farm with his wife, Gertie.

REVIEW US

If you enjoyed reading this book, found it helpful, or would recommend it to your friends, will you do us a favor and review it at one of the following locations?

- Amazon

- Smashwords

- Barnes & Noble

- Kobo

- Apple iStore

- The Crux Publications website

ABOUT CRUX PUBLICATIONS

Crux Publications exists to serve Christian authors who want to publish books that glorify Jesus Christ. We offer the following levels of service:

➢ **Self-Publishing** - For authors who want total control over their books, we'll provide the services that allow them to self-publish under their own name or imprint. These services include print book and e-book formatting, book covers, editorial services, and other potential services upon request. Learn more about self-publishing with Crux Publications at https://cruxpublications.com/diy-publishing/.

➢ **POD/Hybrid Publishing** - Unlike most hybrid publishers and vanity presses, Crux Publications does not charge authors to publish their books. We consider our authors partners, giving them more control over the finished product than they'd have with a traditional publisher. As publisher, we provide our knowledge of the Amazon-era publishing industry to provide the same professional services to self-publishing authors without charging for services. We earn our keep through royalties, like traditional publishers, while authors take the lead on marketing. What sets us apart from traditional publishers is that authors who publish multiple books with us earn higher royalties on subsequent titles. Learn more about our POD Publishing services at https://cruxpublications.com/hybrid-publishing/.

➢ **Testimonies** - The Crux Publications Testimonies imprint allows authors to tell their faith story and submit a manuscript for review. If we accept your testimony, we'll publish it at our expense and pay you higher royalties than traditional publishing contracts. Learn more about publishing your Christian testimony with Crux Publications at https://cruxpublications.com/publish-your-testimony/.

Receive regular commentary on living the Christian life, written by Crux Publications founder and publisher Allen Taylor. Join The Crux community at https://paragraph.xyz/@tayloredcontent

Current Crux Publications titles include:

➢ Finding Peace During Uncertainty: 40 Life-Changing Devotions by Rev. John Clark Mayden, Jr.

➢ Life from the Fire of Afflictions By Patrick Igoche Egah Ikwue

➢ I Am Not The King (A Personal Testimony of My Growth in Jesus Christ) by Allen Taylor

More titles are on the way. You can find Crux Publications at https://cruxpublications.com.